THE WARRIORS

THE WARRIORS

SOL YURICK

GROVE PRESS
New York

First published in 1965 by Holt, Rinehart and Winston

Printed in the United States of America
Published simultaneously in Canada

Library of Congress Cataloging-in-Publication Data
Yurick, Sol, 1925-
    The warriors / Sol Yurick.
        p. cm.

    ISBN-13: 978-0-8021-3992-4

    1. Gangs—Fiction. 2. Violence—Fiction. 3. Teenage boys—
Fiction. 4. Fourth of July—Fiction. 5. New York (N.Y.)—Fiction.
I. Title.
    PS3575.U7W375 2003
    813'.54—dc21   2003042187

Book design by Marshall Lee

Grove Press
an imprint of Grove/Atlantic, Inc.
841 Broadway
New York, NY 10003
Distributed by Publishers Group West
www.groveatlantic.com

11 12 13 14 15   10 9 8 7 6

To my father—
another Ismael in another time

THE WARRIORS

July 4th, 11:10 P.M.

Six warriors crouched in the shadow of a tomb. They were panting after their long run. The moon was shining above them; all the spaces between the gravestones and the tombs were bright but the shadows were hard and deep. Embracing cherubs smiled down on them from the eaves of the tomb, fat-faced and benevolent. Far off, starting from the south and running to the northwest, a solid bank of moonlit cloud looked like a range of mountains. The cemetery was on a hill. Below them were clusters of tombstones, an iron spike fence, a highway, a narrow river gleaming, a long stretch of lawn sloping upward, a line of apartment houses a half mile away, and, between the houses, elevated tracks on which a string of brightly lit trains rattled festively.

3

They listened. They heard nothing but the rumble of the train across the valley. They heard their own gasping breaths mixed with the sounds of rustling leaves.

"All here?" one of the warriors whispered.

The others hissed, "Shh, shh."

They looked at one another suspiciously and shifted a little, all except Hinton who had found a spot in the darkest doorway shadow of the tomb. He sat there, his feet up against one side, his bent back supported by the other.

"What do we do now?"

They cooled it for a while; looked around, recovered from their run. They listened for any strange sound and tried to guess what it meant. Were there other warriors here? Were the police around? They wondered how they could get across the valley to the train.

"All here?"

"Cool it, cool it." There might be a watchman.

Hinton curled further into the shadow. It wasn't so bad here, he thought. He felt almost sleepy, protected because the others were between him and the outside. He was tired. The run had knocked everything out of him. He hadn't slept well for two days—the tension. Now if he could only sleep for awhile. Why couldn't they stay here? It was restful. There was a cool breeze and the grass smelled nice.

From behind the bank of apartment houses a line of fire climbed slowly into the sky and burst into a shimmering American flag. The smiling stone cherubs changed into something malevolent in the spangled light. The whole dragging place spooked them. Illuminated, they shifted positions, milling, bumping, pressing back against the tomb, pushing into the deeper shadows. The flag hovered for a second, was caught by the wind, and began to drift lazily south until it dissolved in a shower of three-colored sparks. In this final burst they saw that Papa Arnold was missing. Someone groaned. They began to count off.

4

"Me."

"Lunkface."

"Bimbo."

"The Junior."

"Dewey."

"Where's Hinton? They get Hinton too?"

"I'm here." His knees drew up to almost touch his chin; his lips were on his knuckles.

"Look at that Hinton; he almost asleep. Man, cool," The Junior said.

That Hinton, he could sleep anywhere. Lunkface tried to look sleepy because it would show how cool *he* was. He reached to shift his hat down over his eyes, but the hat was gone. Lunkface cursed and started to move out into the moonlight to look for it. He was hissed back into place. A series of little explosions sounded off in the distance—firecrackers like the rattle of machine guns. Where was the sound coming from? Hinton closed his eyes tighter; his chin pressed on his knees; his thumb was going to his mouth, but he scratched his nose with his thumbnail instead. Something rustled in the grass. They froze it. Nothing happened. An animal, a rat maybe. Rats eat corpses. That made them feel better; they all knew and understood rats.

Hector said, "Man, we have to cool it here for a while. Maybe Papa Arnold will make it here . . ."

"How's he going to know we're here?" Bimbo asked.

"If he don't come, we move out to where that train is and go home."

The Junior shifted his position and stuck his hand out into the moonlight and looked down at his wrist; he was the only one who owned a watch. "This brother doesn't think it's a good idea. It's going to be midnight soon."

"So?"

"So man, you can't stay in a graveyard after midnight," The Junior said and his voice was hysterical.

5

They all knew about what might happen in a graveyard after midnight. Some of them believed it; some didn't. But it disturbed them all; all except Hinton who buried his face tighter into his thighs which were drawing up. It would be good to just stay here, he thought. It was cool, probably the only cool spot in the whole city now. Just too much trouble to get up and go climbing fences and walk all that open distance to that train across the valley. A few dull explosions sounded.

"We got to get out of here. They come and get you," The Junior said.

That was silly, Hinton thought.

"Man, I got to find my hat," Lunkface said. "That cost."

"We got to get out. They come out of their graves. Everyone know that."

"We stay here a while," Hector said.

"No one elected you Father." The Junior was shrill now.

"You want to tangle about it?" Hector asked. No answer. "Someone has got to be the Father till we get back home. You listen to me. We'll move out before twelve. We have plenty of time."

They waited. They listened. They looked out for the cops, the other gangs, the watchman, while Hector made the plan for getting all the way home.

July 4th, 3:00—4:30 P.M.

It began that afternoon.

Six Delancey Thrones were intent on playing a card game in their clubroom. They were in summer uniform—tight ice-cream pants and red T-shirts. It was very hot. It looked like any other summer day, except that it was the Fourth of July. When they were like this—reduced to boredom, cardplaying—the police were jumpy and the Youth Board Workers were talky, because things broke out of place and rumbled. Outside, in the street, the punks and tots were beginning to blast away with firecrackers. The men looked as if they had always been in that position, nor could they ever move again, except to put down a card, ask for a little luck, curse, or mutter "Man!" as they did again and again. Standing behind them, their bellies pressed against their boy friends' hard shoulders, a few girls watched the play; they

7

rubbed up slowly so that no one should see, or know. Everyone was hard up because Ismael, the Presidente, had forbidden sex for a week. He always barred sex before a rumble; he wanted everyone mean. A transistor radio blasted out rock'n'roll, wailed of lost love, broken dates, betrayal, heartbreak. They welcomed the disk jockey's hopped-up voice biting off the wail-edge of each record because it moved the time along.

The clubhouse had once been a ballroom. A chandelier hung overhead, the revolving kind that used to throw romantic, spangled lights on dancing couples. Toward the back of the room, a three-seat shoeshine stand was mounted on a plywood pedestal. Sitting in the right-hand chair, next to the wall-sized window, his sunglasses looking down over the whole hot and noisy street, was Ismael Rivera. Ismael had the impassive face of a Spanish grandee, the purple-black color of an uncontaminated African, and the dreams of an Alexander, a Cyrus, a Napoleon. He permitted himself no thought—only a vacant, motionless waiting, watching the chill reflection of his own eyes in the blue lenses.

Someone played a card; a chair creaked; the card slapped to the table. One of the girls cursed and was elbowed in her thigh by her boy friend; she had given away the weakness of his hand. Seated on the pedestal at Ismael's right foot, War-Counselor fidgeted. He twitched before any action, but no one in the city was cooler once it started. Secretary, Ismael's man, kept looking at his black-faced Swiss watch again and again, muttering, jittering up and down in beat-time. There was a noise outside; they stopped and looked at the door. A runner came in and walked down the long room to War-Counselor, who leaned forward. The others turned back to their cards again, making it a point to look cool. Squatting, the runner reported. The sound was drowned in the wailing pulsations of the radio. War-Counselor nodded and looked up at Ismael, who might or might not have looked back. The runner left.

The electric wall-clock's second hand swept around slowly, urged on through the heat by the radio rhythms. No one looked at it; it was a point of honor not to look. They knew it was still hours and hours from The Time. More of Ismael's men came in and sat around the edge of the clubroom. Someone picked up a set of bongos and began to flutter rhythms out with his fingers, not loud enough to drawn the radio but faster, to help time along, bouncy enough to make everyone feel a little easier. More girls came in and sat near their boy friends. No one said anything. They were hot, trying to look bored, like on any ordinary afternoon. Now there were about thirty Thrones in the big room and it became hotter. Slowly, the day turned into late afternoon. More heat poured down while the tempo of the explosions outside increased.

There was a knock. It was their Youth Board Worker, Mannie Bernstein. No one wanted him here but they knew he would come; they had planned against it. Mannie's round face looked around the edge of the door. He waited there because even though he had gotten them the clubhouse through the local Merchant's Association, even though he had done so much for them, protocol was still touchy. He had to wait till he was invited in. It was not only a matter of friendliness, he was sure he had won that—but the boys must call the play. Infringement led to resentment: their manhood was delicate and easily wounded. Mannie waited the long seconds—a half minute. They did that to him sometimes; it maintained their identity. Mannie smiled; let them ventilate their hostility. They didn't know what to do and waited for Ismael to give them a sign. Mannie's smile stiffened. As Mannie was about to turn away someone said, "Well, man, come in." The Worker didn't know how Ismael gave the sign. He had been watching Ismael all the while and saw nothing, yet the word had gone out from the right-hand shoeshine chair on the plywood pedestal, flowed down through the whole chain of command till it reached the door. Sweat sogged his shirt. He came in, trying to grin.

The chain of command had to be reversed in greeting the boys. Mannie walked through the room, helloing all the boys and their girls till he came to the throne. But when he reached the Presidente, he saw something was wrong. A tiny gold earring glinted pleasantly against his smooth, black skin and made him exotic, dangerous in spite of the expensive Ivy League summer wear.

"Well, how, like, are we making it, man?" Mannie asked.

The Man didn't answer immediately; further proof that something was wrong. But again, protocol forbade; Mannie didn't ask.

He looked around and recognized the signs: the prerumble card game, the forced coolness, the acted-out boredom, the yawning, the clinging girls showing their anxious sexuality, the bongos muttering like war drums. He turned back to Ismael. Secretary waved his hand, inviting Mannie to sit. Mannie pulled up a chair near the pedestal and tilted back so he could look up at Ismael's idol-face. He began to make conversation to break the coolness, and let him know what was happening. Ismael continued to stare down to the street, but that meant nothing; Ismael never focussed on anything. Someone turned up the radio. The bongos were banging louder. War-Counselor raised his voice to answer Mannie.

Mannie took a special pride in Ismael, who was the jewel of his career, the best and greatest result of some six years of social work with delinquents. But then, how often did one come across an Ismael? If he could keep Ismael straight for another year or so, the boy would be finished with high school, possibly even interested in college. For Ismael had been the brightest star in the firmament of P.S. 42, the rebellious genious of Baruch Laporte Jr. H.S., and, in his two years of high school, he had been

10

the talk, the despair, and the hatred of every teacher. Slowly, Mannie had redeemed Ismael, introducing him to the better things of life—interest in a job, books, a future—and even had Ismael over to his own house. Mannie had channeled Ismael's ego-drives into socially acceptable patterns. Of course, Ismael held tight to the leadership of the Delancey Thrones; the power was too sweet to let go. But the Delancey Thrones were almost a social club now. Time, Mannie thought, give him time. He hoped Ismael wouldn't regress and spoil everything now.

The Worker probed delicately, as delicately as he could without asking directly. Everything pointed to a rumble. But there was no open conflict with any other army. Nothing had shattered this year's truce, even though some newspapers tried to start something by printing false, insulting gossip. No one fell for it. Mannie exhausted the conventional talk about weather, sports, dances, the Fourth. He could have been talking to a mute, or to an idol's stone face. He recognized this role too. It angered him and he fought to maintain his sense of empathy. Patience, he thought . . . Ismael's thin lips didn't move. Preserving his strength against the heat, Mannie thought.

At ten to four the girls began to drift out. By four o'clock only the men were left. The radio announced, in that frenzied, jivy way, ". . . and now, for all the boys and girls of the Paradise Social and Athletic Club, these grooves . . . it's *los* Beatles, boys and girls, banging out . . ."

No one called an end to the play; the game stopped. Some of the boys got up. They left in little groups, trying to look casual. By four-fifteen no one was left in the clubhouse but Ismael, War-Counselor, Ismael's man, Secretary, and a burly guard who lounged against a wall.

Ismael stood up. Secretary told Mannie, "Like we have to cut. Hot. Movies."

"Well now, man, I understand that, man. Where, like, else

11

can you cool off?" Mannie told Secretary and waited to be invited along. No one said anything. "Man, I have an idea about a boat ride we, like, could take in a few weeks," he said to Ismael.

"Later, man," War-Counselor said.

Ismael walked down the length of the room followed by his escort and went out, leaving Mannie alone. He hadn't found out anything. Ismael hadn't even talked to him. He went to the local candy store, looking for some of the boys, anyone from whom he could find out what was happening. None between the ages of fourteen and twenty were around. He got a supply of dimes in the candy store to call up Youth Workers from neighboring armies, and Youth Board headquarters. Maybe they knew what was happening. A kid set off a firecracker right behind him as he went into the booth.

July 4th, 7:00—10:30 P.M.

When Arnold formed his Family, the Coney Island Dominators, he had two mottoes in mind. He had taken them from subway posters. One was, "When family life stops, delinquency begins"; the other was, "Be a brother to him." If they were a family, Arnold reasoned, then they couldn't be delinquents; so he became the Father to all of them. The second in command was the Uncle; the others became brothers. They were closer to one another than to their families; *this* family freed them. Where they happened to live with their parents was always The Prison. Arnold's woman became the Mother, and the other women in the inner circle were daughter-sisters. Members of the outer circle were cousins, nieces, and nephews. When they were taken into the Family, they all swore oaths of belonging.

13

Arnold told his Family not to hang around the meeting place at the candy store today. Only those who were going as plenipos —he, Hector the Uncle, Bimbo the bearer, Lunkface for strength, Hinton the artist, Dewey, and The Junior—should be there. But the Family insisted on seeing them off. He hadn't whipped them into shape yet; they didn't listen to him the way they should to a father.

When it was time, they cut out, leaving the candy-store owner relieved. His fear amused the men. They always threatened to mess things up because they could sense his fright; it made them feel big. Everyone should fear them; everyone would. The chosen seven had liquored up—two drinks a man—for spirit. The radio brought the word—the Beatles record. It was on.

They moved out, a company of about twenty: Papa, Momma, Uncles and Aunts, Sons, Daughters, Cousins, walking their street. The men wore blue, paisley-print, button-down-collar shirts and too-tight black chino pants, high-crowned narrow-brimmed straw hats with their signs: cracked-off Mercedes-Benz hub-cap ornaments—hard to come by—with safety pins soldered in the school shop to the three-ray halo-stars. The appointed mission carried jackets, except for Bimbo, who carried a raincoat in which were strapped two Seagram's pint bottles to keep the men edged. Pedestrians, the Other, quailed before the march of the Family and gave them the wide pass. Arnold's children were hard and held their territory against one and all Other, coolie, fuzz, or gang. They weren't often out in force this early in the day. They swaggered, weaving, prancing, inviting any Other to come on, man. The family band, two cousins, with transistor radios blasting, came along for march music.

They reached the end of their turf and stopped. No one had lined it, like on school maps, and there were no *visible* border guards. The only sign of permanent divisiveness was the usual scum of oily motor leakings, dirty paper, white crossing lines,

14

but the frontier was there, good as any little newsreel guard-house with a striped swinging gate. The eyes of the Colonial Lord were hard and hostile, even though they were allowed free passage today. They couldn't help feeling that old pre-battle nervousness. Their backs prickled; their shoulders went into that old hard-man, can't-put-me-down-man hunch; their stomachs fluttered; they perspired, plucking the tight pants away from their crotches. Bricks might come raining down from the roofs, chains could lash out from doorways as they passed, baseball bats would crack their heads, and knives were whickering.

The delegates put on their jackets; they were the new short ones, buttoning up to the neck and monkey-jacket tight. They fussed, twitching their shoulders, pulling down on the jacket skirts to make them lie better, flicking spots of dust, pulling up on their shirt collars, checking to see if every button was buttoned and every buckle was tight and gleaming while their women fidgeted, helping. Bimbo made sure that the bottles were strapped in well. Their uncomfortable ankle-high, elastic-sided boots were glossed. Their hats sat cocky, high on their heads.

Papa gave the word: they took off the pins from their hats and put them into their inside pockets; there was no point in being antagonistic. Squatty Bimbo, the bearer, armorer, and treasurer, looked around and saw no blue fuzz and, half-surrounded by the Family, gave Papa A. the gift-wrapped package. It was their present to Ismael. Arnold put the small, irregular, brightly striped item into his pocket where it bulked. All the others—Mother, cousins, the sisters, the camp followers—scattered a short distance up and down the street so as not to look like a detachment, so as not to make any of the Colonial Lords, who might be a little funky, panic. The nearest insisted on touching Arnold and patting Uncle Hector, the war leader, on the back.

"Go, Father."

15

"Uncle, keep it cool, man."

"Don't let them jap you, Brother. Don't trust; don't take no shit from them; don't let them lip you down, you hear? Show them who we are, but good."

They crossed the street. The turf felt different; it was Other country. The sun shone as brightly, it was as hot on this side as on theirs. But the dirt fallout in the air smelled different, choky. The people were the same as those in their own land, but somehow not the same. The shadows cast by the hard beams of the late afternoon sun made them feel as if they had plunged into mysterious forest darkness; eyes peered at them from every strange place. They looked back, across the street, where their men were fanned out, looking cool for action. Some of them were rocking to the pocket-radio music; they watched for the enemy Lords, or for the patrol cars to come screaming down the street on them to call it off. But most of all the Dominators watched their own for the first mark of chicken-funk.

An emissary from the Colonial Lords came out of a store, walking carefully, openly, to show them that it was all dignified, friendly, as between equals. Some tot cracked off a string of pop-fire and both leaders jumped. Arnold smiled. The First of the Lords grinned back. They gave one another cigarettes and lit them for each other. Arnold pulled out Ismael's printed invitation, schedule, and through-pass and showed it to the First, who politely said that, man, he took Arnold's word. It wasn't always so. A few other Lords came around with their women and stood, watching. Arnold reached into his pocket and took out the bright package and gave it to Uncle Hector, investing him with the leadership, for the state was truce, yet war. Hector, who was ice-faced, slim, and wiry, took the package and nodded at Arnold. He decided to carry the package in the open.

One of the Colonial Lords, Willie, a little psycho, always pushing for a little fun, started to say "Mother"—a word to fight

16

over. "Muh . . . Muh . . . Muh . . ." and grinned as Lunk-face's fists balled automatically.

"Now man, ain't you got a little present for me?" he said, mock-whining. The girls shrieked and pointed. Lunkface's hair prickled and his fists kept clenching and loosening and tightening. A lieutenant poked Willie hard.

"He don't mean nothing by it. He only talking," but trying to show that friendliness did not mean weakness.

Willie, still not content, said, "No, I don't mean nothing by it. I'm only talking. You know what that guidance counselor say. She say Willie disturbed and we got to understand." He was banged again. Lunkface, short-tempered and stupid, kept stiffening, the action agitating from his fists to his arms and shoulders. Hector tapped him with the brightly bound iron and Lunkface relaxed a little. Some of the Lord women, who always tended to troublemake, pointed them, sounded them, cackling like witches, their faces transformed by old-hag hate.

"Man, are you going to let them walk by like that?"

"Are you going to let them put you down like that?"

"Look at that; he queering you with a *look*."

Obviously, they hadn't been told anything. One of the Lords backhanded a girl across the face. "Cool it, woman." And that satisfied them.

The First, looking bored, said, "Them women; they always troubling."

The Junior nodded agreement; they couldn't be much men not to be able to control the women, but he didn't say so. The Dominators put down the Lords because they were poor fair-fighters; they had psychos and junkies in their rout, and their women were no better than camp followers. They all hung there for one second. Arnold's family watched from across the street. The First nodded at them, but what did that mean? Go? Stay? Bop? Arnold decided that it must be *Go,* and that they would

17

walk in peace for the first time in two years, since Arnold had formed his Family and hammered out his turf.

Uncle Hector began to march. His brothers and the Father followed. They walked it cool, showing they were friendly, but as men do, cool always and fight-ready. It was six hard blocks to the station, in daylight exposed, not in force and not on a raid. They saw a lot of men who might have been Colonial Lords, but none opposed their march. Their discipline kept them cool and neat. A few blocks to their left was the boardwalk and, beyond that, the beach. People were still coming down to the beach, but most were leaving, loaded with beach equipment. Couples drifted toward amusements, looking around, laughing. An old fart with a wicker basket and a fishing pole shuffled by and Hector thought what a great weapon that would make. They heard the faint calliope, the rumble of the rides, the placid wave and crowd-murmur from the beach. It seemed strange to Hinton that on a day as hot and full of danger as today, people should be sunning themselves, drinking cool, canned drinks, eating hot dogs, buttered corn, French fries, and knishes, fretting about no more than how they were going to make it home on a subway jammed with bathers; they didn't know what the world was really like. He was tired already. He hadn't been home for two days. He wished it was After, and he was in the cool shadows beneath the boardwalk, sleeping maybe, or with a girl in his arms. He wanted to see the giant fireworks display later. No more. Cool and in the cool dark; no more than that.

They reached the station. Arnold and Hector talked about splitting up the group, for camouflage, sending them uptown on two different trains, but they didn't dare. The Family didn't know their way around. Who could control Lunkface? It needed two to manage him, and those two had to be Leaders. But it was important that a leader be with each group, and Lunkface was too strong to leave behind. They went up the subway steps in good order: no one fooled; no one jumped up to touch the roof

18

of the staircase, no one pulled pieces of advertising paper loose, no one penciled the signs and no one wrote their names. Anyway, that was Hinton's job. He was the Family artist. Bimbo, the bearer, bought fourteen tokens, seven for going out and seven for coming back. On the station, Bimbo bought them gum to keep cool and chewing while waiting for the train. He also passed out bread crumbs from the dough pile, seven dollars apiece in case they got separated and had to find their way back alone.

In the Bronx, eight boys wearing sweaters despite the heat, and sneering looks on their murderous Irish faces, mounted the crosstown bus. They dropped their fares into the coinbox, moved to the empty back, and sat down quietly. The bus driver could feel the back of his neck ice; he recognized those long-sideburned temples and crew-cut tops. Punky hoods. Trouble. They would sit there for a while, quietly until one would see something amusing—God knew what could amuse these animals—and he would nudge the next boy. They would start to stare, point, whisper, and laugh and finally to shout. Then the trouble would begin. They might pull, and keep pulling, the stop-buzzer. When the bus stopped, they would stamp and keep stamping on the plate that opened the rear door. They would curse to one another, slam windows up and down. Someone would complain, some prune-faced old lady, and he would have to make a stand, would have to stop the bus and go back and tell them to shut up and hope, if they didn't listen to him, at least they wouldn't jump him. Sometimes, surprisingly, they listened. Other times they cursed him in ways he hadn't thought of. Not that he had been jumped yet, but he knew drivers who had been. He tried to keep his eyes on the road and on the hoods. He drove anxiously with his body, avoiding cars and pedestrians, while he worried about the coming trouble in the back.

Boys hadn't been like that when he was young. Tough, sure,

but clean-tough. Nobody killed then. The world was cracking up. If the cops would only use their clubs. The punks just sat quietly. One kept folding and unfolding his arms, sticking his hands into his armpits as though he were cold. Another fiddled with the buttons of his gang sweater while his leg shook up and down uncontrollably. Another looked stupidly at the hot sunset. One even politely made room for a man to pass. And for once they didn't sprawl insolently in their seats. For a half hour the driver waited for the inevitable punk explosion, but nothing happened. Finally, as he was getting to the end of the line, one of the boys rang the bell. *Now,* he thought, but they just got off. They stood quietly, talking as he drove off. Maybe he made a mistake, maybe they were just a school group.

The snotty kid whose father owned the fat Cadillac sat, soft and stupid, between the two hard corporals in the back seat. When they drafted the tank they brought along the owner's son, a no-belonging slave, because they didn't want to get in trouble —not tonight. They half coerced him, convinced him, promised he would be high up in their councils if he volunteered. The kid looked worried, trying to toughen his face to be as bop-brave as the rest of them. You could see him working hard to feel like them, the two flanking him, the two squatting on the floor, and the three in the front seat. But he really knew that they only let him come along because he had gotten his father's long black tanky Cad for them, and because he let them drive it. But he worried; he was a hot driver himself, but nowhere near as wild and terrifying as the boy driving now. The General, staring out at the sun balanced along the rim of the Jersey shore, wondered if they shouldn't ditch the stupid slave before they got to Ismael's rendezvous. The General thought how fine they must look in the tank, took out Ismael's invitation, looked at his watch, and consulted the schedule. They were on time.

20

For the fifth time the General told the driver to cool it, to drive soft and square because if they were picked up, man, they were going to be put *in,* because of you know *what,* man. The driver said that, man, he knew, but his hands stroked the smooth black skin of the steering wheel and his toe eased the pressure on the gas pedal and he said he couldn't help it because, man, if you just *twitch,* man, the hair-triggered gas pedal made you know it, and you knew it because everything was like standing still as they went: Did the General understand that?

The General inspected the driver to see if he was gassed, tea-ed, or liquored. Anxious, one of the men in the back, asked could he drive now? The General wanted to know if the driver wanted some hard-hand head-buster in blue to break a few against his beak? Did he want that? Because as soon as they were cop-stopped, it was a matter of the club touching on their kidneys and asses and the backs of their legs, as they would be straddle-footed and bent over in the far lean against a wall, or against the car. What then? There was no chick around to run off with Ismael's pretty present between her legs. He knew, he knew, the driver whined, and slowed down some more. Why couldn't he have a little fun and drive too, Anxious in the back pleaded. The General didn't answer.

But a few joy-kids, some clean school-snots with all-American crewcuts came up the highway behind them, moving fast and passed, looking out of their doctored junk-heap with the roar hidden beneath the battered and flame-stenciled red hood, looking at the sedate lines of the Caddy. They recognized that here were rivals, and they hooted and laughed at the smooth black mass of gleamy Detroit Iron, pointed them, sounded them and put the men down. Here it was not a matter of chasing them and catching them on foot, and fighting it out. These hot-rodders knew the way tanks went, and theirs whooshed and coughed and growled and the fake old heap came to life and was dwindling up the West Side Highway ahead of them, threatening to vanish in the distance beyond the George Washington Bridge.

The driver couldn't stand the challenge. It was a question of not being put down. The driver touched the pedal, trying to look cool, sedate, bored. He told himself, "Ah yes. Home, James, man," and giggled. The tank hummed a little, and shot forward. The driver felt it, that subtle and exciting touch of power transmitted to his fingers, tingling them. They all wanted their tank to beat the souped-up heap, and they couldn't help yelling, even the General. It would be nice to go by and just blast them, to show them who they were dealing with. Wouldn't that surprise them? Anxious was hunched forward in the back, holding an imaginary steering wheel, which he kept wrenching around imaginary curves violently, lipping car-roar noises.

And at first the heap got no further away. And then they gained on it while the sides of the highway, embankment, and river, ran past faster. The men squatting on the floor *had* to raise their heads to see what was happening. And even with eight in the tank, it moved without effort, with tremendous power, so that the driver felt he had the strength of the world here, and felt it like it was in him, and he almost had more of this power, more, even, than the General. The noises from the car imitator in the back became deafening and his eyes were on his own private road. But the General remembered himself and he told the driver to cool it, cool it, cool it! The Driver kept arguing . . . but man . . . saying that allright, allright, he was slowing up, and it wouldn't do to slow up so suddenly because look what it did to the car, or to anyone behind them. And for one languorous second more his foot was heavy down on the pedal, giving it one last goose before he let go, unable to free himself from the throbbing feel of it.

The General twisted his body, reached into his jacket pocket, pulled out Ismael's checker-papered gift package. He brought it down hard against the hip of the driver, telling him, man, the next time it would fall he knew where. Did the driver want to dispute rank with him? Because he, the General, was ready—right now—to pull over to some private corner and show who had the power here. And the driver slowed down, promising himself a little fun later on. Just in time, because around the curve was the heap parked by the side of the road. The all-Americans were out getting ticketed by a blue fist in a helmet, wild breeches, and too-much boots. The heads of the men on the floor shot back under the rim of the window and the driver of imaginary cars braked his lips. They wondered what would happen if they were intercepted. So much depended on their not getting caught.

The cop, turning the corner, almost ran into them. There were about ten of them. They materialized out of the dusk, looking incongruous, brutal under the leafy, spreading trees. They walked beside the tended lawns, coming at him like the night itself. What were Negroes doing in this neighborhood? Were they an integration group? He'd bounce his stick off their skulls. They all had that same hostile face and he couldn't tell them apart except by size. Were they a Muslim group? His left hand began to tighten on his club. Were they a gang? He read that they never left their neighborhoods; he had never believed it. This was a fighting gang. He tried to make it look as if he were innocently swinging his stick.

It was not so much fear that disturbed him, but the barbaric anarchy of it. He had never seen such groups in this almost suburban neighborhood. Law and order had failed; they never came up here. Could he arrest them for unlawful assembly? Why were they here? Did the trees beyond them and across the street conceal others? What were they going to do? Were they going to beat up the neighborhood teen-agers? Or would they break

23

down the house doors and rape the women? Set off explosives, shattering the Fourth?

They all wore many little brass buckles on their raincoats and point-up shoes. Their hair was straightened, pompadoured high, held in place by wide, shiny black headbands. What was concealed under those short black raincoats: bicycle chains, zipguns, shivs, brick sacks, baseball bats? He gripped his stick a little harder.

The narrowness of the sidewalks forced them to parade past him in twos like a frightening parody of a military formation. He almost panicked into shifting his club to his right hand. But no one strutted. No one taunted. They kept on stepping, marched around him and were past, going quietly, not even looking at him. He tried to look into their eyes and see if they were hopped-up. They were past and it was all he could do to keep from turning around and looking behind him, but if he made a wrong move, angered them by turning, he knew their treacherous weapons must flash. They would be on him, beating and kicking. He was sure they were watching him carefully. He could hear their feet, receding, clicking precisely on tapped heels and toes. As long as he heard them he was safe. But had some of them stepped off onto the grass? Those shiny shoes were indecent on the clipped lawns. He grabbed his stick with his right hand. The thong caught on his left wrist. This was the moment to let loose. He yanked hard, sure that some missile was already flying at the small of the back, or the head. The thong slipped loose and he shifted his stick to a better swinging grip. He couldn't stand it any more and turned his head.

The whole gang had moved on. They were in very good order, marching away till he had trouble seeing them in the dusk as they went in and out of the darkness cast by the trees. He stared in the direction they had gone. The last thing he saw was the twinkling buckles on their shoes. When they were gone he walked slowly after them, slapping his stick in his left palm. He

24

wondered if he should report their presence on the beat when he phoned in.

The car in which Ismael Rivera sat was not old and not new, not big and not small; certainly, it was not too sporty. It had been driven carefully, skillfully, all the way from Manhattan. The distance to the staging area was not far but they rode south across the Brooklyn Bridge and through Brooklyn, up along the interborough chain of highways into Queens. They had driven down side streets, through tunnels, over elevated highways, past cemeteries across which they could see the high buildings which seemed to spring from the graveyards—greater and more distant mausoleums. They stopped in many neighborhoods, but only for a second, a minute at most. They held quick briefings and drove on. Sometimes they merely exchanged signs with some scout as they went, people were celebrating the Fourth; the sound of explosions was building up slowly. The sun hung hot and set-heavy, balanced on the spire-points. War-Counselor looked at Ismael's face, nodded, and said, "They'll know it soon."

Now they were time-killing, driving around quiet streets where large houses were lawn-flanked and quiet; only birds were seen. Secretary said, "The richest people in the world live around here." They listened to the car radio playing *pachanga* music; if anything went wrong the announcer would relay a *request*. Soon it would be dark enough to head for the Bronx where they would drive across town to the assembly place in Van Cortlandt Park.

Ismael sat in the back, relaxed, smoking a cigarette, his face motionless behind those lenses. The sides of his eyes were shaded by the heavy sidepieces that swept around his head. But he had been watching and seen it all: the streets, the cemeteries, the trees, the fine houses, the waters of Long Island Sound, and the clean arc of the bridge over those waters to the Bronx.

War-Counselor was busy going over the arrangements. There

25

were so many things to keep in mind: some gangs had chickened; unexpected representatives were coming; could they be put in the same place as the canceled soldiers? He kept looking at maps and consulting notebooks. He wished he could have thought of it all himself, but that was why he was the Counselor and Ismael was Presidente. It was that way since he had been with Ismael, five years now.

Secretary, who sat beside the driver, had been looking out the window at wonderful and unaccustomed sights, goggling at the splendor of the city, dreaming dreams, hoping for things he might have someday, given a few breaks. Certainly, he understood, if things went well with Ismael's big plan—and when had Ismael ever failed—he might, just might, make it. "Man," he said, "that's the way to live. I want one of them," pointing to a half-timbered house they were passing.

War-Counselor looked at Ismael, nodded, and said, "You should want to throw rocks at it."

Secretary understood what Ismael meant and his resentment that always lurked beneath his surface surged. He saw himself tearing it down with his hands. Still, secretly, he wished Ismael had found it good and he couldn't help longing again, wistfully, and dimly seeing himself in the coolest, most expensive clothes, lounging around in a vague, but impressive house with a rich T.V. interior. Outside, there would be a long, long car to leap into, gleaming and heavy with a lot of chrome. He would have a slender, huge-breasted wife, a blonde, encrusted with shining stones; she would shimmer in shining dresses; she would have many children—boys—for wasn't he a man, didn't he have *machissmo?* But she would remain always desirable. Much money would be present, piles of bills and precious stones. It was all unclear and satisfying.

"But you have to admit, man," Secretary said to Ismael, "that they know how to live."

26

"This is the nearest you are going to get to it," War-Counselor said for Ismael, who knew how to keep them hating.

They turned along the sweeping, graceful approach ramp that bowed over everything as it led to the bridge.

It grew dark. They were all assembling, reaching the ends of the transportation lines, converging on Van Cortlandt Park. They came by subway, cars, buses; some walked. They followed Ismael's schedule and they followed Ismael's guides who wore white ice-cream pants and were stationed at the jump-off points. They avoided the usual park entrances. If the cruising cops noted a lot of white pants—well, it was hot, wasn't it, and it was this year's style. The cops had enough to do taking care that the celebrations didn't get out of hand. One boy was already in the hospital because some firecrackers went off in his face, and it was still early.

Warriors poured in from every part of the city, from New Jersey and Westchester. They were met and directed along chosen routes that led, wherever possible, along hidden paths through forest, between hills, wandering among bushes, always away from the promenades. When two gangs were known to be at war, they were given separate routes as far apart as possible. Ismael's couriers escorted them, passed them from one liaison man to another along the lines of communication, directing them carefully through the dark cover in which only the white pants of Ismael's men were visible.

As they moved uneasily along invisible roads through black fields they were comforted by the knowledge that all around them plenipos from most of the city gangs were converging on the meeting ground.

Benny the scout, Ismael's man, stood on the edge of the highway that cut through the Park watching for the signal from the guide on the other side, who kept a lookout for cars. When there was a lull, he gave Benny the word by blinking his flashlight. Then Benny directed the waiting men across. He squatted behind a clump of bushes, staring into the unbroken blackness for the signal. Behind him crouched six delegates from the Morningside Sporting Seraphs, potent and deadly, with a fine war record. Their faces shone a little under the lamplight from the road. They wore big, bulky caps slewed off to one side. One of them looking at the arcs of July Fourth fire springing up in the blackness around them, and listening to the explosives, said, "Man, wouldn't this be a good time for them to come down to kill and drop that old A-bomb? I mean boom; but good. No one even notice."

"Man, you're too stupid. You see nothing, you hear now? Nothing. You dead before that boom finished. Like that. Boo-dead-oom. Maybe quicker."

"Well, what do I care? Serve them right. *All* the mothers would get it. I mean all them others, and us, we'd be in the same boat. Some show. Man, wouldn't you like to see that old bomb?"

"*You* wouldn't see it."

"Well, maybe for one second, like. Some rumble. Boom, man."

"Man, you something else. Stupid."

The flashlight across the road blinked. Benny passed the word and the Seraphs kicked off, bent and weaving, running furiously, bodies horizontal, knees kicking, holding imaginary rifles like movie soldiers. They were across, gone, and into the darkness in two seconds. Benny waited for the next group to move up. Beyond the bush-clump, cars hissed by, their headlights stabbing at the back of the bush.

Arnold and his Family were led through the dark land. Arnold brought up the rear, guarding against a sneak attack. They squelched across a little muddy turf—it had been raining a few days ago—and Hinton stepped cautiously; where would he get money for another pair of shoes? Lunkface protected his hat against the branches. Hector kept brushing his clothes. It was unfamiliar here, and frightening. The effect of the drink was wearing off and they were jumpy and irritable.

The runner turned them over to Benny and went back to get the next detachment. Benny turned around and saw Hector. Now Benny had trouble with Hector when they both lived in Ismael's territory. That was a long time ago when they were both bopping tots. He was startled when he saw Hector; he owed Hector something hard. Hector, in turn, thought he owed Benny a little man-to-man. Benny was tough. He never gave ground to any man but his officers; that came under the heading of discipline and did not detract from manhood. But now was not the time; this was not the place.

They faced one another. Benny had to look away for the signal. Lunkface, who was closest, recognized what was happening and laughed, sneering at Benny's face-loss. The lull in traffic came. Benny waved them on. Hector didn't move; he knew Lunkface had seen it. Papa Arnold stepped out a few feet on the highway, but came back. Lunkface watched them carefully.

"Man. You. Move," Benny told Hector. "You want to ruin everything? You want to bring the troopers down?"

Hector started to go, but Lunkface put his hand on Hector's shoulder to hold him. And so Hector said, "Who tells me to move? No one tells me to move. When I'm ready, man, then I move."

"You're holding up the operation," Benny told him. Even if Hector was going to sound him and demean his manhood in front of the others, Benny had made up his mind to take it. There would be time to settle things later. He was a man and the big part of his manhood now consisted in being one of Ismael's

29

Army. That meant discipline and taking lip when you had to, for hadn't everyone in the land heard of Ismael? Benny saw it was too late to move now; the cars had come up and were sweeping by. Lunkface was moving around to Benny's side and he got himself set. Arnold caught Lunkface's arm. "You let your uncle roll his own."

Headlights spangled the backs of the bushes, filtered through, and speckled their faces suddenly with shifting leaf patterns. Far off, crackers fired and a row of dull explosions walked around the horizon. Hector and Benny faced up. Hector waited and then began to move across the road, satisfied that his honor had not suffered. Benny took hold of his sleeve and told him to chill it, to wait for the word. Hector looked at Benny's face. He looked down at Benny's insulting hand holding his sleeve. He looked back at Benny's face. Lunkface was bouncing up and down a little on the balls of his feet, muttering something that no one could hear, something almost animal-like, exciting himself for *that moment*. Bimbo came up and looked carefully at both faces and waited. "No one tells this man to move," Hector said.

"Ismael tells you to move," Benny said, invoking authority, letting go of Hector's sleeve, realizing that he had made a mistake.

"Don't listen to him," Lunkface said. "Go."

"You, child, shut your mouth." Arnold said. "Don't lip. Don't sound."

Behind them, another column had been moved up.

Bimbo whispered, "You can't do anything now. You have to cool it, man."

"I know him," Hector said. "He knows me."

"I know you," Benny said.

"Talk. Go. All this talk. Go, man," Lunkface agitated. Arnold nudged Lunkface in the ribs with stiffened fingers. Lunkface grunted. "Next time, the eye; you hear?" Papa said.

30

They stood there long enough for honor to be satisfied. Arnold knew that the whole operation could be jeopardized and he said, being big about it, "All right, you'll fair-it later. Now call it, children."

"You running?" Lunkface wanted to know.

"I'll run *you*," Arnold told him. And Dewey told the Lunkface to still himself and wait.

The lookout from the other side of the highway signaled frantically, wanting to know what had happened. He was ready to fire the blue alarm flare, but when the lull in the traffic came, Benny gave the word. They ran across. Around the far bend the first sweeping bars of headlights came down the road. Further down, they could see other groups crossing the same way, running quickly and secretly. They went down a little hill, past the signaler, and were picked up by another scout in white pants who took them through the black field. Far ahead and a little above, where another highway ran, headlights swept along. They came to their place on the damp plain. The sky was coming alive with fire.

A red flare climbed slowly from the middle of the field and hung in the air. It meant they were all there now.

Ismael Rivera's car had circled the complex of park roads, looking for a clear space between the bunches of moving cars. They had gone around the meeting place two times. Ismael looked down there and saw nothing but a flat, black plain, and that, he thought, was good. No one was visible. No one was lighting up, for he had given the word that there was to be no smoking. And it was a credit to his organization that none of his scouts or none of the groups had been seen crossing the highways. He knew what to look for and still he hadn't seen it. Could it be smoother?

The driver shot ahead of the cars around him and drove in

clear darkness now. It was the third time around. Soon the nearest headlights were left a quarter of a mile behind. About a quarter of a mile ahead, a band of little red lights receded, dancing in formation as they bounced over potholes. The red lights swept around a curve and disappeared. Ismael's car slewed around the curve and the headlights behind were blocked out.

Ismael nodded to War-Counselor. War-Counselor passed the word to Secretary. Secretary told the Chauffer. The Chauffer edged to the road rim fast and his lights blinked a message. About twenty sentries came out on the concrete and were picked out by the lights; they stood fifty feet apart. The car screeched fast and stopped; one of the sentries opened the doors. Three of them got out; the car started again, going so fast for a moment that the wheels spun on the pavement, gripped, and the car roared off.

The three of them were escorted down the embankment, following the dim white pants. Although the darkness seemed to hold nothing but damp, unfamiliar smells of vegetation, the sounds of insects buzzing, and the rustling of grass and leaves, Ismael knew that they were all there, a thousand strong. As he went, Ismael received whispered reports from the scouts. There were ambassadors from almost every major fighting gang in or around the city.

Ismael was taken to his place. He began.

July 4th, 10:30—10:50 P.M.

The glorious Fourth was reaching a new crescendo. Even though explosives were forbidden, all around the Park rim, Roman candles were going up, sheaves of many-colored light blazed, explosions canonaded in an almost steady rumbling barrage. Faintly heard strings of crackers machine-gunned and blinked away. Sparklers burned for a little while like stars. Rockets exploded into a thousand patriotic shapes: heroes of American History, Presidents—Washington in lights to the west, Lincoln in nebulous clouds auroraed down toward the south, Kennedy danced in the northeast—historic flags blazed. The Statue of Liberty shimmied in an air current.

Ismael stood on a little rise—like a pitcher's mound—in front of a stand of bushes which concealed him from the roads. A ring of flashlights had been stuck into the ground around him and tilted up so that he was illuminated. His eyes stared through the cold blue glasses and he felt all the eyes stare back. He remembered an advertisement—something about how someone's life was saved by flashlight batteries: Whose life would they save tonight? He heard a responsive murmur coming from the darkness, but it might have been a change in the wind, for all he knew. He stood there, dapper, the coolest, wearing the neat, simple, Ivy League clothes; he shunned the too-tight fit, the surplus of buckles most of the men wore. His hat sat neat and square on his head, and except for the one earring that glinted in his ear he could have looked like an advertising man. Did they understand what he had done?

They waited in the pool of dark. Bracketing them, two rows of highway lights strung away and the cars sped by, faintly heard, known mostly by the flash and turn of the headlights shooting off into the night over their heads. Further back were the lights of apartment houses. Here was The Man with the Idea, who was rumored to have twenty-one expensive suits in his closet and as many pairs of shoes; the Man with an arsenal that could outfit a battalion. Who did not know Ismael?

Ismael knew he had about ten minutes to get The Word to them. Their attention would stand no more. He heard hands slapping at mosquitos. He had to make it simple and he had to make it dramatic and he had to give them just enough to bring them out, roaring. Once he really got them going his cadres could keep them that way for a long time. He imagined this moment many times, he thought again and again of everything he had to say to them. He rehearsed how he would distill his knowledge into this moment to which the Idea had brought them. Though his face remained, as it always must, impassive, he felt the terrible surge of power, that throb when he had to release it in one scream. The sunglasses masked it. He knew he didn't dare orate to them; they were always talked at, and they had learned long ago not to listen. Then too, his voice was not strong; shouting, it would not even reach to the end of the black field. He had stood in front of the mirror and ranted, gestured, made faces, but he knew he couldn't showboat like a Castro. What he said must be simple, for most of them were not quick of understanding. What he said must be spoken quickly, for most of them had no patience. What he said must be put strongly, more acted than spoken, for they had to be hooked to stand and hear. He knew they moved there in the darkness frightened by their strange surroundings, ready to break and run, always nervous when they were away from their own turf.

Two hundred yards away, Lunkface moved restlessly in the darkness and wanted to know, irritably, when the Man was going to begin, or was he going to showboat there all night, posing his sweet clothes in the flashlights? Stolid Bimbo whispered to wait. Nervous Hinton shifted, unable to squat comfortably, feeling eerie there in the darkness. How much of this strangeness could he take? He was on the verge of terror and it was only the feel of his family around him that kept his mask tight.

Ismael stabbed his forefinger toward the circling city lights and turned all the way around, his rigid arm pointing, accusing.

Hector whispered, "Listen to the man." Ismael started. They could hear none of it yet, only see his arms moving.

Ismael talked. He talked, hard-lipped and softly the way he always did. He told three signalers squatting in front of him; he told the swarming darkness and the far-off shifting headlights, and he told the city lights and the silly-kid fireworks in the air and the blinking plane lights crossing overhead, challenging everything. The three signal men heard his first words, turned and passed it on to the other communicators who repeated the Word, relaying it, conversationally, deeper and deeper into the night. There was no other sound now.

35

Ismael told them what he was. They knew him. He had come up and taken over a fall-apart gang that had been dying for ten years through changes of personnel. He had the reputation of being a fierce fighter, a cunning planner. Who led his forces better? He had challenged, conquered, and assimilated a number of other gangs and won face for himself and rep for his fighters. Then he had made his men into mercenaries, hiring out his army to help other gangs in their rumbles. What army had more experience? What army had more discipline? He had given them new, magic signs which had force. He could now muster three hundred men, counting auxiliaries. What army had more equipment and money?

They knew him. His face was there for all to see. His big blue lenses mocked them all with daring equanimity.

In the darkness they all nodded.

Why were they here? He gestured again, finger pointing, arm stiff, pivoting on the mound. He told them they were here because of the Enemy.

He reminded them about the Enemy, the adults, the world of the Other, those who put them down. The courts and the prisons and the school-prisons and the home-prisons; these put them down. The newspapers put them down. The big-gang men put them down because they would never take them into the rackets. The ones who charged too much for everything put them down. The pushers working to hook their people put them down. The ones who held all the good things of life and misered it out— cheap living, televisions to dream with, the overpriced and easily repossessed cars, the fall-apart, cheap-slick clothes, all to be earned by breaking their backs for the rest of their lives—these put them down. And the worst were the people who were supposed to be *their* friends: the social workers, the Youth Board men, teachers, all the guidance people who spoke words like community centers, organized dances, sports, outings, reading, the Mobilization for Youth, the Career, this Haryou shit, Peace-Core fags; promises like church . . . They all remembered what a big fist his older brother used to be. Now some pentecostals had hooked his brother; his wife dropped children once a year and he clapped hands and body-rocked to that Jesus *salva* shit, didn't smoke, repented for being put down, dog-worked, and smug-smiled all the time. All worse than tea; dreamier than junk. War on poverty? He had the real war and he gestured again, fist shooting out, elbow locked, finger pointing, turning slowly in place.

They knew. They nodded.

He told them they were all lost, lost from the beginning and lost now, lost till their deaths. If they were lucky, they would make a quick end and if they were not, they would drag it on, child surrounded, like their parents, being nothing more or less than put-down and fit-in machine parts. Some of them would go junkie, or psycho; they knew what that meant. Sure, they could be pushers, or policy runners, but that fed the machine too.

They nodded. They knew it.

Or did they think they might make the big escape by stealing, working their way up into the rackets? There were no rackets for them; hard work was not rewarded; all they would do was to sneak-steal till they were caught and busted and spent a third of their lives on the Inside. And if the police didn't chill them, the racket boys would ice them. Did they think they could make it? Ismael anticipated them. He reminded them: If they were hard, where were the old hard boys now? Where were all their wasted brothers and all the busted heroes? But how much more *hombre* was an *hombre* in a group than a man alone? They had to know it.

Most of them agreed. A few hardheads and a few kooks kept shaking their heads because they *knew* they had the stuff to lift themselves into a new destiny. They would make it out of the strongness of their fists, the insanity of their drives, or because they were much man: wasn't America full of such stories? Even the blazing skies painted heroes who had made it the hard way and told them about the power of violence. A little luck . . . that was all it ever took.

He reminded them; it was hopeless . . . unless they listened to him. Arnold nodded wisely and wished he had thought of it all that way himself. And he believed he just might bring his children in. The Junior kept edging back at the words the signal man passed on: he didn't understand them and shook his head violently, saying that man, he didn't dig any of that jive at all, and what was more, he didn't want to hear any more of it. Arnold nudged the Junior. Bimbo, the bearer, waited, ready to agree with whatever Arnold and Hector agreed with. Hinton fought his wild terror, but managed to look as icy as Ismael there, frozen in that pool of light in the Park darkness. Lunkface listened to the words and began to see where it was all heading and understood that here was the Man, the leader they had all been waiting for. His face began to twist with excitement and he kept nodding in time to the moving lips he could just make out. Hector, always alert to threats from the outside and internal discipline, kept half-listening to the words, hardly hearing them, watching both his men and the surrounding groups, barely visible in the darkness. Dewey heard.

What was to be done, Ismael asked? Ismael said that at any time there were twenty thousand hard-core members, forty thousand counting regular affiliates, sixty thousand counting the unorganized but ready-to-fight. That was about four army divisions. Did they realize what that meant? He told them. With the women it would come to a hundred thousand. A hundred thousand! They had their arsenals. He told them about the big dream he had. One gang could, in time, run the city. Did they know what a hundred thousand was? There were only about twenty

38

thousand fuzz. Why should the biggest power force, one hundred thousand, in the city be put down by the Enemy, the Other? They would tax the city and tax the crime syndicates. What was to be done, Ismael asked, and waved his palm-down hand over the great area of darkness.

Brotherhood, he said. There were one hundred thousand brothers and sisters. And before he heard the protesting murmurs, he told them, "Now we're all brothers, I don't care what you say. They make us think we're all different so we rumble in colored gangs, white gangs, Puerto Rican gangs, Polish gangs, Irish gangs, Italian gangs, Mau-Mau gangs, and Nazi gangs. But the iron fists break all our heads in the station house the same; and when that judge, he looks down on us and says Youth House, reformatory, or Riker's Island, or the Pen, he is treating us the same; they treat us like we, one and all, had the same mother, and they fuck our mother and that's what makes us brothers."

He shot out his arm. The fist was clenched. His other hand was over his arm in the Gesture and he turned, more slowly than before, gesturing at the whole world around them.

And for a moment they were all one. Two hundred yards away The Junior felt it; he was one of a vast and comforting throng, and the terror of being in a strange place was not so frightening for a moment. Lunkface could see the backed-up headbusters being beat in their own prison cells. Hector could think, now, in terms of handling big platoons, companies, battalions of men, who could move in swift, devastating raids. Hinton would be able to walk long distances without having to fight. Bimbo dreamed of being deferred to. Dewey hoped that it would be an end to hanging around, waiting in the morning for the night to come, bored, always bored. Papa Arnold wondered how he could get close to Ismael. They yelled and Ismael held them for a second. They were formed into a soothing bubble of power

39

and warm community. They yelled together stood and made the Gesture in every direction. But it could only hold for a second; too many things probed at the skin that united them all. What Ismael said got garbled in the passage because the communicators and the listeners to the Word could hardly understand its power or meaning, and so saying it right, or hearing it right wasn't so important. The dissident elements couldn't stand it. Some gangs had too much rep; some too little. The Nazis hated that crazy nigger prancing up there. The Muslim gangs thought he was a traitor, a Puerto Rican, and so really white and where was the white man you could trust? Their harsh hatreds could only rest for a second at a time and they must break out, knowing only to offer violence before it was offered to them. The psychotics could never maintain discipline, could never be grouped too long with others; they were too restless. Most of the others could never dare place themselves far from their dreamy wants of kicks, power, women, clothes, cars, and honor; some of them had almost been won back into the world, were beginning to believe in the way things were and couldn't dare to sacrifice the joy of belonging. The frightened shied away from it because they could almost see, palpable out there, beyond the park ends, the terrifying shape of the opposition, those massed apartment-house lights, the now-innocent fireworks sounding and flashing in the air; only a little sign of how the world could come down on them.

Someone slapped at a mosquito; a jumpy warrior misinterpreted the sign and struck back. A fight broke out. Groups began to bop in the darkness. A lot of them, not trusting the situation completely, had brought their own flashlights and began to use them. A whorl of violence swirled, and expanded outward. Gangs reformed, shattering that holy instant of universal unity. A few men, always prepared, undid garrison belts from their middles and prepared to start lashing, buckles out. Someone put down someone else's mother. A few of the gunbearers began to shred the gift wrappings off the token guns to feel protected; they pointed the power, still afraid to use it, probing the surrounding darkness.

The fights were still scattered and the liaison men were trying to stop them. Some fights were halted momentarily, but the guides had to linger to make sure that Honor was not offended. Movements were interpreted as being hostile, and purely defensive blows were struck. The fights kept dying down and starting up again all over the field.

Father Arnold called his children closer together. The seven of them formed into a circle, each facing outward. Lunkface, as always, wanted to break discipline and go rushing off into the darkness, swinging, smashing, but Arnold and Hector flanked him and held him in place. They just waited for the noise and the roar to die down, hoping they wouldn't have to fight.

Someone, unable to take it, fired a shot. A piece of leaf fluttered down from the bush behind Ismael. Secretary tried to pull him down. Ismael, warrior and leader, disdained to cover himself. His face was composed; his cool smile mocked them and challenged their stupidity. The blue eye-disks looked at the seething, flash-lit blackness; he heard the muffled shouts, the sounds of blows, contemptuously. His calm, he thought, would have a cooling effect; they must come to their senses.

But it had gone too far for one man to stop. The fighting was general now; peace and universal organization were irretrievable in this violent blackness. Arnold's sons held tight, checked by Hector. Here and there other groups refused to break peace and fight, but stood firm and were bumped against in the blackness. The fighters pounded at Ismael's men, identifiable in their ice-cream pants. Some of the wilder ones, the truce-breakers who had never trusted in the first place, who were jealous of Ismael, were unslinging secret chains wrapped around their waists.

41

There were more guns than had been accounted for. The gift tokens were all shredded free of their wrappings; bright flakes of colored paper fluttered in and out of the flashes of light, candy-bright in the middle of the night. Some jokers lit firecrackers and threw them around.

And someone tipped the cops. Maybe a passing motorist had seen it all. Or worried Youth Board Workers had sensed what was happening. A frightened warrior, or one of their women, feeling that old rumble-fear, had told. And they were coming down on them in prowl cars now. They heard a siren from a long way off, but unlike the city, now there was no place to run and hide, no doorway to disappear into; only the unfamiliar field, the blackness itself, or the bright highway. The siren grew louder; other wails joined it; the sound was a cliché—they had heard it so many times—but paralyzing. They couldn't run—which way, where, would they go? Only Ismael's men knew the way out. The red lights on top of the prowl cars were blinking. Police car after police car raced down both roads, flanking them. And who could have betrayed them but Ismael? Who could have gotten them there where they would all be together, easy to hand over, who but Ismael?

And so they presented their tokens of allegiance in a different way than they had intended. From all around the field they aimed their guns at the circle of light. They fired. From those distances, and in the confused lighting, only two bullets reached. Ismael's body was thrown back through the halo and held up by the thick stand of bushes. One hole was unnoticed in the dark material of his suit. The other shattered one blue lens so that Ismael's face seemed to wink at them contemptuously before he slumped. The flashlights illuminating Ismael paled suddenly as a great blaze of headlights and spotlights poured down on them from two sides.

Heaving in viscous agony, their bodies writhed, moved by the shower of light to a moment of furious action. They pounded at one another, not only at enemies, but at friends, as if only terrific motion could make them feel less frightened. Light bathed them. Even the most well-disciplined gangs wavered. Some of them broke entirely; they began to run, and running, smashed into other men and stopped to slug. Others ran in circles. Light drenched them. More police cars were coming up, rushing to the scene along the parallel highways, screeching, turning toward the field, stopping, and aiming their headlights and spots onto the field till it became unbearable. They were all naked in the light, inundated. And, slowly, their movements began to stop. They paused. They waited. A field full of panting boys were fixed in the lights, aware only of the blazing gush that poured on them, drowning them, and aware of the complete, terrifying, shore of blackness that lay beyond those lights.

July 4th, 10:45—11:10 P.M.

For one moment everybody was still. The beacons on top of
the police cars kept turning and threw patches of red into the
mass of light. Ismael's body slowly slumped, sinking out of
sight, disappearing as if he were being dragged to the bottom of
the sea. Some kid sobbed; the sound bubbled, startlingly clear
throughout the great patch of silent brightness. Then, someone
who had seen too many movies tried to frighten the fuzz with a
few shots, trying that old trick of shooting out a light. The headbusters replied with a warning on the bullhorn. But the wild
man, some uninvited psycho, safe among the mass, had to show
off his heart and fired again; the bullet caught one of the spotlights and shattered it, but it seemed to have no effect on the
blaze at all. The fuzz fusilladed warnings this time, trying to

44

scatter the bullets widely over all their heads. The bullhorn kept roaring and echoing, warning. But a panicky cop, trying to shoot low enough to really frighten, fired into the mass of boys and someone—shot—screamed.

The scream started them. The mass roared and they began to run. Some of them ran from side to side and back again, smashing into one another. Gangs began to fall apart. One warrior held the end of a honed-link bicycle chain and, grinning madly, swung and swung around, safe in the center of a ten-foot, silver radius. Most of them took off in the directions they thought they had come from. Some of them ran to the south and collided with police detachments working their way through a field to cut them off across their flank. A small mob, trying to make their way westward, to the Broadway subway line, blundered into a line of cops and cars. The cops waded into them and began clubbing wildly, driving the kids back into the field. A loudspeaker kept saying, "Stand perfectly still and you won't get hurt. Stand perfectly still and you won't get hurt." Another speaker said, "Line up. Hands up. Line up." A mass charged to the east, ran into the glare, got caught at the police line and were beaten off, but some got through and into the darkness; the police didn't bother to follow. A detachment of kids tried to pretend they were surrendering, and then, when they got close, charged the cops. But a few bullets fired in front of them broke their discipline and they stopped. More prowl cars and paddy wagons were arriving. The fireworks hadn't let up.

Motorists were pulling up and getting out of their cars. Cops were trying to move them on. Traffic was beginning to stop and jam. Onlookers crowded behind the police lines to watch the fun. A handcuffed, hair-banded Muslim being led to the paddy wagon, palm-pushed by a thick-faced shover, saw the O-eyed audience and went a little crazy, broke loose and plowed into the suckers, screaming because he was made out such a fool in front

45

of their eyes. He knocked down an old lady and was biting into someone when the cop banged him to the ground and kicked him along the asphalt, scraping his face bloody while someone said, "The little savage, give it to him." Ismael's chauffeur tried to tank his car through to pick up the Leader, who he didn't know was shot. He knocked down and killed a surrendering Seraph, brushed a policeman, and bogged in a soft patch, furiously miring himself deeper till the busters pulled him out and bounced a few off his skull. A Delancey Throne, his ice-cream pants shredded and his privates showing, was telling a bull to unhand him; he was coming, but just take your mothering hands off, got slapped into the paddy wagon.

Arnold's Dominators waited, held together, stayed by Hector, stunned by the great fight, held in place by the double bank of police lights. They stood still when the shots were fired. They stood still when the mob broke. They waited for the word to move. Hector, looking cool and dangerous in the lights, full of heart, just kept holding his hand high, even though Lunkface wanted to start fighting: and The Junior knew it would be so simple to just start running. A minute passed. The riot was general now. When Hector was sure the police were busy, he hand-signaled for them to move out. Hector vanned and Arnold rear-guarded. They walked north toward the stand of bushes where Ismael had been. As they moved, they stepped up the pace to a half-crouching fast walk, having been drilled in this pre-battle movement by Papa Arnold and Uncle Hector. Another loud-speaker started giving orders to the boys, yelling at groups that were trying to make their escape, telling them that flight was useless; they were surrounded.

"Then man, what're we running for? They got us," Hinton said.

"Son, you don't know a thing. That's talk. Down and keep moving," Arnold said from the rear. "Follow your Uncle."

Lunkface moved, clench-fisted and bop-stalking, hoping that someone, anyone, would get in his way, or that some lone cop would get close so that he could hit him a few times before they were caught. Hinton wondered if it wasn't better to just stop and wait with the others to be rounded up. The cops would *have* to let them go: how could the jails hold so many people? A fourth loud-speaker started giving orders. Cops were shouting directions and yelling to one another to look out for this or that bunch trying to escape. The voices met and fused into a general, crushing roar and every statement became meaningless; mere noise.

Arnold's Family moved north, screened, for the most part, by the herded boys standing around and waiting for the cops to come for them. They made it to the stand of bushes. They passed a bunch of Ismael's men standing around the body of their leader. They wanted to stop and look, but Hector yelled for them to keep moving. Arnold in the rear should have known better, but he *had* to stop and look at Ismael's face. One of Ismael's men asked him what did he think he was looking at, and before Arnold could say anything, he was surrounded and being pounded and down. Bimbo, just ahead of Arnold, didn't notice because of the noise; he was moving after the others faster now and they were into the black bush clumps and out of that terrible dazzle. It was cooler here. It was a relief to get free from the light and they moved faster. Branches tugged at their knees, but they were trotting now, getting further and further away from that zone of brilliance. And then they were clear of the bushes and following after Hector who was vaguely outlined by the beams of the jammed-up cars at the highway junction ahead.

They reached the embankment where the highways joined. Hector, outlined by carlight, shimmering in the mercury lamps, waved them down. There was no point to waiting around. Hector gave the word; they would charge across between the

47

stopped cars and make their way toward the left, west, in the darkness. Hector told them not to be frightened, to keep together, and when they got to the other side of the highway, they would link hands and make their way through the blackness. Hector knew, vaguely, they had come from that direction. Anyway, the Park had to end and they would be out of it soon.

They ran across the highway and down the embankment on the other side and into the darkness. Behind them, seeing them run, the motorists began to sound their car horns insistently, trying to warn the police. The men, panicking, ran faster. The ground was wet and getting softer and they seemed to be moving into a swamp. They had all seen movie heroes sink into quicksand; was there quicksand here? But they all knew that if anyone started to sink, the thing to do was to get a big branch and lay it across the quicksand hole . . . but who would have the courage to stop? Their shoes were not made for running and were getting soaked, ruined fast here. Lunkface wanted to stop and light up a cigarette, but Hector knocked it out of his hand; was he crazy? That was the word that always infuriated Lunkface, and he was almost ready to fight, but Hector was ordering them to link hands and follow him. He kept Lunkface close to him.

They moved fast, half-running through the darkness, getting further and further away from that great bubble of light, not knowing where they were going, drifting north, west, then east, and finally, they were lost, moving up and down hills, through marshy land, panting. The loud hums of big insects whirring by startled them. They slapped at stinging bugs. Were there wild animals here? Wildcats? Wolves maybe? Certainly snakes. What kinds? They weren't sure. Pythons? Rattlers? Frogs sounded, crickets chirped, louder than firecrackers. Dewey stepped into a small water-filled hole and shouted. They hushed him and ran around him, pulling him through even though Dewey was afraid

48

of alligators. Whipped-back branches hit and stung their faces too. Lunkface got a mouthful of wet leaves. Hector almost shrieked when he walked into a spider web; he made frantic brushing moves in the dark air; he had heard about black widows, even huge, man-eating spiders; but he kept his mouth shut and kept Face, and grabbed Lunkface's hand again. Bimbo felt the raincoat catch and wanted to stop to disentangle it, but he was pulled on and the coat ripped. He felt for the bottles; they were safe.

It seemed as if they kept moving for a long, long time; they wanted to rest badly. Hector wouldn't let them. They were gasping; their sides hurt; they charged up a rocky hill, slipping, falling, getting up again and again; The Junior tore the knee of his pants; and they were at the top and running across a firm-grounded sports field and the park ended suddenly in a sidewalk and street. It was a long, peaceful street with thick-boled trees, not too busy; a few people walked along it. Across the street, behind an iron-spiked fence, was a cemetery. A bus was heading toward them, and farther off, Bimbo saw the revolving red eye of a cruising cop car and he pointed. Hector had an idea and waved. They bolted across the street, climbed up and over and down into the cemetery. Moving carefully, they weaved among the tombstones till the street was blocked by the tombs and gravestones. Hector gave the rest sign by dropping to his knees. They all fell down and panting, they rested in the shadow of the big tomb on the crest of the grass sloped hill.

49

July 4th, 11:10—11:45 P.M.

The Junior got jittery; it was taking too long. Lunkface was angry over his lost hat and The Junior was making him nervous with that ghost talk. Dewey wondered if it could be true. If— things—*did* come up from the graves.

Hector said, "Now we cool it here for a few hours and then, when the shit is off—"

But The Junior whined in a panicky voice, "But I *told* you. We *can't* stay. Them graves might open up and . . ."

And they all huddled closer together, but got no comfort from the nearness. Arnold might have helped; Arnold was their Father. But the Father was gone now.

It takes about an hour, an hour and a half, depending on the subway service, to get from the top of the Bronx to Coney Island. But not if you are crouching in the dark shadow of a tomb. Not if the little fat stone cherubs on the tomb press their cheeks together, and their smile becomes more and more evil as the hour evolves to midnight. And not if every cop in the city might be alerted and blockading, not if every gang truce in the city is off and every gang's hand is raised against every other gang's. Coney Island is about fifteen miles away; it might as well be fifteen hundred, because everyone between here and home is ready to come down on you. And if there is no plan yet, if they are falling apart as a Family because the Father is gone, and they have to be there, home, *now,* then it means that an infinite distance must be covered. And that was why Hinton, because he didn't believe in ghosts, couldn't see the necessity of leaving this nice, cool place on this night, and walking that far across all that empty space, exposed in the moonlight, to get to the subway. There was time yet.

"Man, I'll take myself off and make it by myself," Lunkface said. "I'm not going to hang around this place."

Things rustled again. There was a watchman. Were the fuzz sneaking up? No, cops came clumping in loud and didn't care. Was it another gang? Whose Motherland was this anyway? No one knew.

"Well, if it's the spooks that's bothering you, children, why we'll move out and cool it in another way," Hector played it chilly, with scorn, hoping that they wouldn't be foolish; that they would agree to stay. But even Bimbo said he didn't want to hang around.

When Hector saw the way it was, being rational about things, he said all right, they would restructure, they would elect, they would move out as a Family—because if they made it like a mob—they knew what happened to mobs. They agreed.

The Junior said, "But man, we have to hurry it."

They elected. There was no question that Uncle Hector should

51

become the Father for the time being. Lunkface wanted it for himself and voted for himself and glowered at them when he didn't make it. They didn't even vote Lunkface for Uncle, because you could never trust what he was going to do. They gave the vote to Bimbo who was cool, unimaginative, steady; a good man to have by your side in any bop, jap, or rumble. Lunkface became the third in command, eldest son, and that, to some extent, satisfied him; to give him anything lower would have caused trouble. He was sixteen, a little liquored up most of the time, but six foot one and thick and broad and strong. The second brother was Dewey; he was seventeen and had been with the Family for a long time and was reliable. The third brother was Hinton. Hinton was the artist because he had a talent for caricature and could draw fancy letters; he carried the Magic Marker and left the sign of the Dominators wherever they went. They all thought he was a little psycho because when he got the fighting madness, even Lunkface was a little afraid of him. But that was Hinton's secret: not having the strength or the heart, he knew that everyone feared the flip, and so he psychoed once in a while and they gave him room. The kid brother was The Junior, a sort of mascot, really still a tot, but with heart. They liked to match him against tot-mascots from other gangs to see the little ones fight. He was not only the youngest of the group, but his name was *really* Junior, and he always carried a rolled-up comic book or two in his pocket. After the election, Hector had Bimbo pass the bottle around for one drink; Lunkface took two because he was angry over his hat and the election. Hector told them to smoke, but light up under the cover of their jackets so that the flame wouldn't be seen. He told them to smoke one cigarette, no more; to keep cupping their hands over the light, to lay it low till he could come up with the plan of action. Lunkface thought that they should discuss plans democratically, but Hector pointed out that he was the Father and it was Lunkface's duty, as oldest son,

52

to follow. Lunkface was angry, but he didn't say anything else.

The thing to do was to get down the hill, over the fence, across the street, across that highway and river, up that long lawn, through the barrier of apartment houses, onto the subway, and go home. That was one way of doing it. The other way was to phone their Youth Board Worker, Wallie, tell him they were in trouble, have him come up and get them in his car. Then, Hector told them, since that square, Wallie, was trying to get in good with the Dominators, he would think, ah, at last the time had come to do the Family a favor. They knew different, of course, because Wallie was an Other, so they might as well use him. They agreed with that. They would go down, near the subway, and call the joker and have him come. If he didn't come, they would take the train and make it home. They weren't sure where they were; they weren't sure where the train went; downtown and uptown; that was enough to know. The Junior was getting nervous about their hanging around here and tried to rush them to finish their cigarettes.

Lunkface asked who had Power? Who was packed? No one. Father Arnold had the .22 pistol-token to give to Ismael, but by now Arnold was probably in the paddy wagon. No one had come loaded because they had obeyed the truce instructions to the letter. It made the distance seem longer now; how could they go through all that territory without being equipped for any action? And what if the Youth Board square didn't come; what then? Hinton asked why they couldn't stay here just a little longer? They ignored him.

"Man, did you see that Ismael? He's not so big now. Choom. Right through the eye," Lunkface said.

Hector said, "Ismael was a big man and he had the big idea." He bowed his head in tribute.

Lunkface didn't think so; the idea wasn't so much; it was even obvious.

53

"We shouldn't desert. Arnold might come," Hinton insisted.

"Man, even if he got away, how's he going to know where we're at?" Hector asked. "Use the head." And then he said for them to get out their pins. They would wear signs; they were moving out as The Family.

Hinton asked if it was wise to walk around the city looking identified and for all the world to know who they were and what they were.

Hector got angry and said that they moved as a Family and that meant wearing their signs, or not at all. Hector thought it was just something Hinton might have said. Hinton was still new; in the neighborhood a short time; in the gang only about eight months. He looked at Hinton in the shadows: Hinton's face was cool enough, his head resting against the stone, looking almost bored by the whole thing, his eyes closed, his fingers making doodling motions on the marble. Well, it was probably just that Hinton didn't have enough sense of tradition and Family, Hector thought. He would get it in time. Lunkface said that if Hinton was chicken, he might stay here for the night and let some other gangs or the fuzz catch him, or, for that matter, the rats might mistake him for one of the corpses and finish him off. Hector told Lunkface that counsel should not be mistaken for cowardice and not to sound his younger brother that way, unless Lunkface wanted to deal with him. Lunkface said that this son was sorry, but there was an edge of mock in it. Hector accepted it as a complete apology to avoid trouble now.

Hinton said that it wasn't a matter of funk, but that they, the Other, would all know them.

"You're not that famous, son. You are not The Ismael, man."

"But we got the marks of a gang . . ."

"How will they know what gang we are?"

"That's not the point, man. They're after all the gangs around this territory. After what they saw, they will pick you up if you're between fourteen and twenty and look wrong. And tonight, everyone looks wrong."

Hector said that they would wear the signs, and anyone who wouldn't, could make it back alone. Hinton understood that the discussion was over.

They took out the pins and gave them to Hector. They kneeled in front of Hector and he pinned the signs on their hats. Lunkface was furious because he had lost his hat and he wouldn't ruin his jacket with pin marks, but Dewey said that Lunkface could wear a handkerchief around his head and they would pin to that. Hector wore his sign in front of his hat; the others wore the pins on the sides of their hats.

Hector told them that if the Youth Board joker didn't make it, they might go as a war party, because it would mean that *all* truces were off, the shit was on, but good, and the police would be all over, coming down on them, and you wouldn't be able to trust your own mother and father. They all laughed; it was an old Family joke.

Hector told Hinton to leave their mark. Hinton took out the Magic Marker and put the family sign on the tomb, Dominators, LAMF, DTK and told The Junior, "I leave this for them ghosts."

The cloud bank had moved a little nearer. Hector tapped Hinton on the shoulder. Hinton, knowing that Dewey was watching the area ahead for enemies, came out of the comforting shadow, bending low. He sped down the hill in short rushes till he disappeared in a shadow. Then Lunkface was tapped and moved out.

55

July 4th–July 5th, 11:40 P.M.–12:45 A.M.

At the bottom of the hill, near the fence, the gravestones were set close together. Dewey said, "Man, they got them shoulder to shoulder here."

Hector made The Junior rear guard to bug him: he crowded close and said, "Don't talk like that, man." They moved on down. The Junior gave a little gasp when he had to step on a grave to keep from falling; his foot sank a little into the fresh soil. Crouching, they could move without having to rush from shadow to shadow, screened now by the tombstones.

Bimbo said, "Look at that." In the faint light from the moon, they could see someone had spelled out *Spahis* across a long line of headstones, right above the R.I.P.'s.

The cemetery ended above a street. There was a drop of

about twelve feet. Hector sent Hinton along the fence line to see if there was a place where the Family could squeeze through without having to climb over. Hinton was being tested because he hadn't wanted to wear the insignia. Didn't they see how wrong it was, Hinton thought? He moved along the last line of gravestones, looking over them at the fence and the street below. The moonlight shone on railroad lines, a narrow river, and on the parkway and the long stretch of green lawn sloping up to the apartment houses. The elevated tracks were just beyond. Hinton had once lived around here; his family was always moving around, never staying in one place more than two years. Off to the left, about a half mile away, there was a bridge over the river.

Hinton couldn't find an opening in the fence; they would have to climb it. No one was walking along the street; only a few cars went by. If they jumped from higher up, people in the cars wouldn't notice them poised on the rampart. He found a likely place to climb over the fence. The drop here was about three times the height of a man, but seemed higher. He went back and reported to Hector.

Hinton led Hector and the men to the place.

"Why so high, man? We'll get hurt jumping."

"If we jump from any lower, they could see us, Hector."

"But we might get hurt. We can't carry any busted ankle home. Find the lowest place. Lower, man."

"The way this son sees it . . ."

". . . is not the way we'll do it," Hector said.

"All right, Papa," Hinton said, angry.

"Father knows best," Hector intoned. "Am I right?" Hinton didn't answer. "Am I right?"

Hinton nodded and smiled.

"Look at me when I'm talking to you."

Hinton looked at Hector.

57

"Smile better."

Hinton smiled better.

"Don't let me see your back teeth when you smile, son."

Hinton modified his smile.

They waited for about fifteen minutes; when the prowl car came and passed, Hinton was the first to go. Hector was still testing him and he knew that he couldn't show any signs of chicken or resentment; what if they were to leave him here? He went through it cool, taking great care to look unconcerned. The fence was easy; how many fences had he climbed, some of them as high as twenty feet? He stood balanced on about four inches of concrete ledge; he could almost feel the fence pushing outward on him. It seemed too far to jump, even though it was only about twelve feet high. So he didn't look, knowing when you were scared it was best to think of the thing you are going to do after. Balanced on the ledge, he looked up and down the long street till there were no cars. He turned toward the cemetery; the boys were hidden. He panicked for a second and thought they had run away, but he knew better. He lowered himself till he was hanging and let go. The drop knocked the wind out of him and he almost fell to his knees. He split the back of his right shoe, but it held together by the strip of binding leather at the top. He turned and ran across the street, skipping to keep from losing it. His thighs still ached from the long run. He ran into the shadows of sidewalk trees. Behind the trees, down a small hill, there was a big water tank casting big black shadows; beyond, at the bottom of the dip, next to the little river, he saw the rails.

Hinton turned back. He could see Lunkface posing on the wall, his back to the fence. Hinton stepped out of the shadows and waved. Lunkface didn't bother to lower himself. He grinned and jumped down and showboated across the street. They came one by one. The Junior was last; he jumped just before the signal because he was scared. They laughed. He landed and fell forward on his palms, scraping them; the comic book popped out of his pocket. The jar also broke his watch. He began to run across the street but they all pointed at the comic book and shouted. He turned, saw it, hesitated in the middle of the street . . . and *had* to go back and get it. They began to point up to the cemetery and yell that the ghosts were coming, laughing at his terrified run, till Hector quieted them.

They started walking north, toward the little bridge, trying to keep in shadows. It was further away than they thought and they walked for a long time till they came to the corner and turned right. Walking, the shoe didn't bother Hinton so much. They were on East 233rd Street; The Junior said that it was a long way from home. Hinton had once lived on 221st Street, but he couldn't remember if it had been in the Bronx, Manhattan, or Queens. He had lived all over.

Bimbo wanted to know if they shouldn't go on, one by one. Hector said they moved together. After all, if the police stopped them—well, they weren't doing anything, were they? But Hinton knew first thing Law would inspect their J.D. cards and how could they explain what they were doing so far from home? It was a little hotter down here—no wind cooled it like up in the cemetery. When they crossed the bridge, the strip of park and highway, and went up the hill, they came to two-story houses and the apartment buildings. A few blocks more and they were under the elevated tracks. The street was empty; all the stores were closed. There was a phone booth next to a shut-down newsstand on the corner. Hector said he was going in and call up Wallie, the Youth Board Worker.

Bimbo asked, "Is it smart, man? I mean, after tonight, they're not going to go along with us. I mean, man, this was the big one. Too much, and now they know they have something to be worried about."

Lunkface was against calling up too: "What do we need him for?"

But Hinton thought that Wallie, the Worker recently assigned to them, was a good man. "Wallie took a lot of lip, but he bore up," Hinton said. Lunkface insisted that none of them were any good; the Family didn't need anyone at all. Hinton explained that with every cop and warrior surely on the alert, possibly with road blocks, check points, heavily guarded enemy turfs, they might have to fight their way through, fist alone because they had come unpacked, except for Arnold's Power and that was gone now. They had a whole city to march down till they got home. Hinton thought that the others didn't understand what was ahead. They would see. They weren't being smart; they were showboating, advertising. It was no shame to be smart, cautious, like Arnold. Hector was always trying to show what a bigger man than Lunkface he was. But Lunkface was the strongest; you never made a fool of him openly, not unless you were ready to bop. There weren't many men who could take out the Lunkface, so you outwitted him in other ways, like Arnold did. So Hinton only said that they had to phone to have an easy ride.

"We need Wallie because this younger brother don't feel like any two-hour ride in some hot subway, man. I like my style and I like my comfort. Besides, how's he going to rehabilitate us if we don't give him a chance to help and understand us?" Dewey asked.

Lunkface liked that. And Hinton added that Wallie was their man, almost one of the gang now, wasn't he? Hector was sure now he would telephone. He deposed the men in shadowed places.

Wallie didn't sound sleepy; that meant he was awake—as if he had been waiting for the call. That worried Hector, Wallie wanted to know where they were.

"We're in the Bronx, man," Hector said.

"Hector, what are you doing in the Bronx?"

There was a lot of static on the phone. Hector felt hot, naked, a sitting duck there under the booth lights; it was dark outside and they could see him so clearly. He opened the door and it felt a little cooler when the booth light went off. He wondered if the static meant that the conversation was being tapped. He read about taps in the newspapers; some kind of noise meant they were listening in, but he couldn't remember what kind of noise it was supposed to be. "We're out for an airing, man; like we just had to see the *country* tonight because it's so hot. It is always cooler up in the North, so we made it north." It couldn't be a tap; how did they know he was going to call from just this booth?

"Were you up there in that big gang rumble? Were you mixed up in that, Hector? Where's Arnold?"

So they knew about the fight on the plain already. That wasn't good. He wondered if he should tell Wallie about Arnold. The Father, Hector thought, was probably sitting in a headbuster headquarters and they were giving him the old twenty questions which went, "Why did you . . ." and then, Pow with the back of the hand, and "You're not dealing with those bleeding hearts on the Youth Board now, you little black motherfucker." Slap, slap, slap, keeping their hands in his face. Or they'd crowded Arnold into a bugcrawly pen and he had to fight for a little sleep-space. Hector decided not to tell Wallie. "We're on a street called two, three, three, man, up in the far-out end. I mean, like we would like a little sightsee through the city as we come home. Drive us?" They couldn't possibly know he would come to this booth.

"Are you all right? Who's with you? Are the boys with you?" Wallie asked.

"You're so inquisitive, Wallie. Man, I don't think you're accepting us."

"Don't give me that shit, Hector," Wallie tough-talked.

Hector grinned; they were training Wallie, but good. "Like

there are a few of us here, one or two, and like it's two thirty-third street, and are you like coming, Wallie?" His throat felt raw; he had to get out of that phone booth.

"Two hundred and thirty-third and where?"

Outside the men had faded away and were holed up in the shadows; he couldn't see anyone. A prowl car drifted by and Hector turned his back to them, but not fast and not too jerky; not far, just enough so they wouldn't see the pin shining in his hat. He could feel them giving him the hard look as they passed, but he was one man making a call; what was so bad about that? The spot-car passed.

Hector told Wallie, "It's by an elevated train."

"But what's the street?"

"You're so inquisitive, man."

"Do you want me to come or not?"

"I called you, didn't I?"

"How am I going to get to you if I don't know where?"

"Like some grave called White Plains Road."

"How did you get all the way up to the ass end of the Bronx? You were mixed up in that rumble, weren't you? Are you in trouble? Did you do anything? Some boys were killed."

"No. Nothing serious. We didn't do anything."

"Anyone in prison?"

Or could they tap any booth at will?

"For Christ's sake, stop asking so many questions. We're in trouble here," Hector yelled and was ashamed he had shown strain. He would fix that Wallie for making him show weakness.

"I'm coming. Don't move. Was anyone hurt? Don't move. Just stay where you are and I'll come. An hour. Don't move, do you understand? If it takes me a little longer, don't worry. I'll be there."

"I'm cool. I'm waiting. Come on, lover."

"Don't move . . ." Wallie was saying as Hector hung up on

him. He was sweating when he got out of the phone booth. Between a building and the elevated tracks, he could see the cloud front had come up on the moon and the white-tipped edges of the clouds were swallowing the light. What had Wallie meant by its taking a little longer? How much was longer? Why should there be an extra wait?

"The man is on the way with the excursion bus," Hector went around and told each of them. They were placed where they could see one another. A train passed overhead, going uptown. One came downtown. They fidgeted in the darkness. Hector holed up where he could see all the other hiding places. After a while he went out and over to The Junior to ask him what time it was. The Junior's watch said 11:41, but that seemed wrong. They listened and found the watch wasn't running. That fucked everything up, Hector thought; how much time had passed? He went back to his hiding place. He wondered how long it was going to take and tried to figure out a way of knowing how much time had passed. He tried counting, but that went too slowly. Two of the men, Dewey and The Junior, began horsing around. Hector crossed the street and ordered them to stay in the freeze. Dewey asked how long they had been waiting; it was hours, he was sure. He was bored hanging around. How much longer was it going to take? The Junior said no one could be expected to be perfectly still; besides, there were no cops anyway. Hector said to maintain discipline; whose fault was it they were out of the cemetery? That quieted The Junior because he was a little ashamed.

Hector inspected Hinton's cave. Hinton was sitting in a small, dark alleyway between two stores, his knees drawn up to his chin, staring at the wall ahead. Over his head a sign in luminescent gold paint announced that the territory belonged to Golden Janissaries. Hinton pointed, "Can't be hard—they have a bad Crayon."

63

Hector had never heard of them. He asked how it was going. Hinton said it was going. Lunkface was fidgeting in a store door, squirming, wanting to move it, bouncing in and out of the shadows. He kept leaving his place to go and talk to his brothers. Hector ordered Lunkface to get back and returned to his own hole-up. Bimbo came over and asked how long did Hector think it took to get up here from where Wallie was? Hector said he wasn't sure, but it shouldn't take too much longer.

"It took us more than an hour to get up here."

"But that was on the train."

"Well, he's got a car. That means he should come twice as fast, doesn't it?"

"It don't mean that."

"I mean a car should go twice as fast."

"It should, but it isn't on the straightaway. Stay cool. He'll come," and he remembered what Wallie had said about it maybe taking time and not to panic. So he had Bimbo break out the bottle. Hector took a drink; Bimbo took a drink. Bimbo went all around and gave everyone a drink. That killed the bottle, but Bimbo put it back inside his raincoat—you couldn't tell when it would be useful.

They waited. Another train passed. About a half-hour passed. Two couples passed, the boys leaning all over the girls, playing their hands on the house fronts; one couple was walking with their lips glued and their eyes shut tight. The men thought it was funny; the lovers didn't even know they were being watched. One of the girls carried a portable radio and it played rockabilly love songs. But Lunkface had to play cute and come drag-dancing out of the shadows and strut by them very close, looking carefully, insolently, at the girls. The boys stepped free to look him over. Lunkface kept swaggering. The boys wanted to give Lunkface what he was looking for, but the girls held them back. The lovers let Lunkface go striding on, high, and the Family didn't have to come out and stand up for him. One day he was going to do that, Hector thought, and the Family was going to let him get what he deserved; he had it coming, but good. Lunkface turned the corner and disappeared and the boys relaxed and kept walking with the girls. One girl's hand kept holding on to her boy's ass, squeezing, and that excited the Family. The other boy kept turning his head, looking back at the direction Lunkface had taken. That clown, Hector thought again; he would have to penalize Lunkface when they got back to the territory. What if Wallie came while Lunkface was gone? What if the fuzz showed?

The time kept dragging. No other trains came for a long while. Did the trains stop running after a certain hour? He began to wonder if he had made a mistake in calling Wallie after all. They could have been almost home. And how much could you trust him—any Other, for that matter? If Wallie knew where they were—and tonight—could the Other overlook a rumble like this—how sure of Wallie could they be?—could they be sure this wasn't a trap—what if the cops were tipped—what if they were just around that corner—if Lunkface had danced into their arms? And after all, the trains went downtown; that was the way the hometurf lay. If they were on that train, they could always look up which way they had to go, what transfers they would have to make. It was really simple. And now the Lunkface had called attention to them. What if the boys were part of some army, those Spahis or these Janissaries, and came back with reinforcements? A prowl-car siren sounded from a long way off and Hinton got nervous until it faded. Why had Wallie insisted that they shouldn't move—some kind of trap? No. That wasn't the way these Youth Board jokers moved. But what if they had decided to clean them up, once and for all—what if it all *had* been some kind of trap to get all the gang leaders, all the hardest rocks into a net—what then? Well, if that was the case,

65

Ismael had gotten his, but good. But now it would be a matter of cleaning up the ones who had gotten away.

Lunkface came back and was laughing. He went over to Hector's hiding place and said he had gone around the block and passed the couples again. "They didn't even see me. I walked by so close and they didn't even see me. You know, they're all sitting on a stoop, their mouths slobbering and that eyes-shut jazz, and one of them had his hand inside her pants and was feeling the old you know what, man. We could take them chicks away."

"Get back to the hole and wait," Hector told him.

"Man, it wouldn't take long," Lunkface said. "They're around the corner and all we have to do is indian up and jap them quick and take those cunt. We could go back down to the park and do the job and be back before that Wallie would get here. We *owe* it to them chicks to show them how *men* operate, don't we?"

"Get back and wait. We're in enough trouble as it is."

"Or man, we take them with us! We could do that. And if that Wallie, he don't like it, why we could just take the car too."

Hector told Lunkface to make the girl out of his hand and to cool his warrior in the dark waiting place. The Lunkface did what Hector said, but he was hot and didn't much like it.

They waited. Hector began to trust Wallie's word less and less, perhaps because no one's word should be trusted. And the longer they waited, the more exposed their own hiding places seemed to be. Hector saw a prowl car drifting by, about two blocks away; in the other direction, a block or so down, a beat-bull strolled by. They seemed to be casual enough, but—on the other hand they could be moving in on them. Arnold would have waited it out, Hector thought, and now that *he* was the Father, he would play it wise, old, and cool, too. Clouds began to float over the moon, and for a while they could see it, but its light was dimming, breaking through less and less till after a while the moon became completely blocked out. It slowly grew more airless, closer, and the thickness, mugginess, became palpable, and Hector could smell something faintly smoky—smog, maybe.

Hector was hot and sweating now; the sweat made him uncomfortable, but he didn't take off his jacket in case he had to move fast. He waited. A sudden rill of perspiration running down his side made him jump. He realized he hadn't heard any fireworks going off for a long time. Did that mean they had stopped shooting off because the neighborhood was becoming loaded with Law? Hector made himself think it was all right; traffic was holding Wallie up. But, on the other hand, where was the traffic this time of the night? If Wallie reported them, it might take just about this much time to set the net, surround them, trap them, but good. From uptown far off, he heard the faint sound of a train rumbling. Hector thought he would give it till the train after this one—that would be enough time for Wallie. If Wallie wasn't here by then they would know, definitely, that something was wrong and they would cut out.

That patrol car passed, but it seemed as if it was a block nearer. Or was it a different hunt-buggy—going a little faster than he thought it should. Some older men came by, never noticing the Family hiding—or did they *pretend* not to notice. Could they be the plain clothes?

As the train came in, Hector couldn't take it; he stepped out and gave the signal.

They all came out of the shadows, ran, and were clattering up the stairs and vaulting the turnstiles while the furious change-maker was screaming at them, shaking his fist from behind the booth bars.

They turned and gave him the upyourself sign. The change-maker started to come out of his booth. Bimbo brandished the bottle. The coin flunky ducked in and down in his cage.

They ran up the second flight of stairs to the train as it was ready to close its doors. Lunkface threw himself between the doors and held them open as, laughing, the others slipped under his arms one by one into the train.

But Hinton turned, took out the Magic Marker and went back to the advertising signs and wrote the Family name, big, across everyone else's marks—and he downed the Golden Janissaries and the Spahis for good measure, and strolled over and ducked under Lunkface's arm while, a few cars up, the conductor was shouting at them to let the doors alone.

July 5th, 12:45—1:30 A.M.

They thought it was only a matter of taking a long, dragging ride in an empty train. The shit was off here; the subways were relatively neutral territory; you only had to fear the fuzz. They might even sleep a little. But the train was crowded. People were sitting in every seat; the aisles were jammed.

"Maybe it's that old night shift," Dewey whispered to The Junior. But something was wrong with the riders—all of them. They were eerie, weird, something else. What was it? The doors closed. The clothes were wrong, but not with all of them: the faces were—off, but not with all of them: the eyes—sitting or standing they all looked asleep—but the eyes were *open*—yet closed. The Dominators moved together. Wild and crazy looks flicked over them. They tightened their enclave, shutting out the

Other to feel safer. Men drooped from the poles or hung from the handholds; women lolled, their hair uncombed, gazing laxly into space, sitting with their legs loose, spread out; people leaned on one another in twos or threes; some of them concentrated on empty space; others peered at newspapers; some of them were bent over sheets with rows of figures, peering intensely, making marks with pencils, muttering to themselves; some of them, pushed, took a few seconds to see the Family, frowned at them and their bust-in noise, and shifting their position, looked away and seemed to forget they had been shoved.

The place chilled the Family. They looked into the car behind; it was crowded, too. They tried to see what was ahead; too many people were in the way. Hector asked a squatty man with a flattened nose and thick eye-ridge flesh, standing next to him, whether this train went to Coney Island. The man turned slowly, looking up from a sheet covered with printed and penciled figures, as if being dragged away from something very important, as if barely having heard the sound, let alone the words—and looked at Hector's face, focusing slowly, slowly, the eyes becoming not-dead, perhaps even recognizing another face, trying to think about the question very hard, but not making it and not caring to. Hector repeated the question. The man finally seemed to understand what it was they wanted of him, shook his head, not so much at the question but because it was too much trouble to answer, whether he knew or not, and looked away.

A woman was seated near them; her head was on her hand and her mad stare conned them, but she was Another Thing; she didn't see them. They wondered again, and consulted among themselves, trying to figure it out. Two heads bent together, the hairs almost touching, over a sheet full of tables and calculated carefully, gently tapped other numbers while their lips moved prayerfully, the sounds lost in the roar of the moving train.

Then, all of a sudden, Hinton figured it—they were all coming from the race track. Norbert, his mother's boy friend, was always putting something of his own, something of his mother Minnie's Relief check, anything he could get hold of—stealings even—on the horses. Alonso, Hinton's half-brother, who was a junkie, looked a little like this after he had ridden his Horse. "That's hooked, man," he told the men: "But the fix is almost over. Horse players," he said and then they understood it. It was just that they had never seen so many suckers in one place, and never without the bookie.

"They're back from the track. That's up in Yonkers. Trotters. And man, if they're anything like that old Norbert, they're toting the day's losing and planning how they are going to make it tomorrow."

"Man, they go so far for it? Why don't they patronize Your Neighborhood Book?" Dewey asked.

"If, they're like Norbert, they *do*," Hinton told them. "Two tracks, flats in the day and trotters at night, a bookie, and maybe two, three policy numbers a day, depending on what them dreams tell him, and a game of cards or craps into the early morning. Norbert, he likes his action, man."

"Well, they sure look like Something Else," The Junior whispered. The Family looked around contemptuously; they were free of slave habits.

The train came to a station. 225th Street. Where was that? Hector gave the word to The Junior, the reader, to get over to the map and decide where they were, where they were going, and how they were going to make it back to Coney Island. The Junior elbowed between two men whose clothes were grease-spotted and stunk of garlic. It was hot here and the creaky fans weren't getting rid of the heat or the smells. He leaned over the head of a wrinkle-faced monkey-woman; she wore an old-lady straw hat with fake flowers around the crown, a dress printed with soiled flowers; a little pince-nez was balanced on her nose;

71

The Junior thought he smelled dried piss. She looked up at a spot on the ceiling and her head bobbed on her skinny neck with the train movements but her hand was steady on the racing form and she marked endless and intricate little signs, completely filling in the margins, without even looking down, talking to herself with a knowing little smile. The men recognized it for the junkie's smile when they promised themselves a fix. Dewey pushed over beside The Junior and looked close at her. Her eyes, huged-up by the glasses, looked directly at Dewey, who looked back at her for a second out of his thick-rimmed glasses, and the men had to laugh because they eight-eyed each other, but she didn't even notice Dewey. Dewey, he bowed. She didn't see. He waved his hand in front of her face. The men laughed and Bimbo buried his face in Lunkface's shoulder because it wasn't polite to laugh at an old lady that way. Then Dewey, he made faces, but she only saw some secret future.

"Man, look at the Duchess. She's saying that, 'Well, I put two on Goalong, and Goalong, he comes in and that pays me four-fifty. And then I put it all on Comeonin, and Comeonin, he goes along. And then she is really flying high on that old horse. Only it comes out different in the end," Hinton said. Dewey got tired of the play and came back.

The Junior was having trouble with the map. He had seen city maps before, but this wasn't like any map he knew. It was abstract, as if the contours of the city had been worn smooth. No feature of the landscape was clear, and he was sure the relationships were wrong; it looked more like some wrong diagram, not like a map at all. Where was Coney Island? But after a moment he found where they had been and he found where they wanted to go. He could, if he had time enough, work it in from the ends, his fingers carefully following the train lines, unraveling the threads for each line, BMT, IND, and IRT, because they were printed in different colors. He had it worked out that they were on one of the IRT lines. They came to another station. No one got on and no one got off.

Lunkface saw the Little Man Everyone Pushes Around; he had saucery, lid-chopped eyes and looked like a moron. He had thick, pale lips closed over his moving mouth, like he was chewing with his front teeth. His black Borsolino hat was too big and sat just above his eyebrows. Lunkface nudged the men and gave them the nod and they laughed at the way the simp looked.

The Junior was having difficulty with the center of the map. He had it figured out that they were on the wrong line; they had to change somewhere, or they would never get to where they wanted—where? All the train lines met in the center of the city, and got tangled up there, and then emerged again, and everything ended up where it should end, but The Junior was having trouble following it; he moved his forefingers slowly along the lines trying to bring them together, but train jolts kept knocking his fingers loose. He tried to rush it so he wouldn't look duncy in the eyes of his Family.

The face under The Junior's chin was talking right up at him. She sounded like Another Thing because she didn't say words, but a high, croon. He muttered, "What, Lady?" at the piss-smelling Duchess, but she kept on sounding and frightened him. He looked back at the Family standing in their little clump, all waiting on him, and he was sure they were laughing at him. He was supposed to be the big reader, and so he left the map before he had it figured, and fought his way back. Hector asked The Junior if he had the route worked out. The Junior said of course he knew what to do; to have said otherwise would have been to lose face.

The train began to slow and stopped where there was no station. The train moved a little. The train began to inch along, gaining momentum, jerking them, and then stopped again suddenly. No one but the Family seemed to notice. Those others

73

were still coming off the kick because, as Hinton saw, they were figuring, trying to do it in imagination with figures what life didn't do, because figures never lied, did they? New numbers worked out what they would do next time; told them what they had done wrong. But if logic and calculations made it . . . Hinton knew it all: no one limousined home. Norbert, his mother's boy friend, stumbled in, busted every time, the money spent, and told Minnie how he should have really won it only . . . And then he beat her up for lipping him because he really should have won it, but . . . Hinton knew the whole story. Some fireworks were still going outside. The players didn't turn to look and didn't care. Their celebration had happened at the track and the only sparks they cared about were the kind you saw from pony hooves. Their explosions were always in the future—if they could only figure it—when there would be no "but for . . . ," no more "someday." Hinton knew all about it.

Dewey nudged and pointed; "The Professor," he said. They looked at an old man wearing a stained homburg, a wing collar, a striped tie, ragged-lapeled jacket and open, velvet-collared coat in spite of the heat. He leaned his head on his knobby hands which were supported by a rolled umbrella. "Man, how can you thread yourself so queer?" Dewey asked. "Look at that cocoon."

The train had stopped again. The motor under their feet kept humming erratically. The fans spun, but it got hotter and hotter because there was no motion-breeze blowing in. The warriors sweated in their dirty clothes. They looked out into the darkness. "What's keeping this train here?" Lunkface wanted to know.

"Yeah, what for do you pay all them taxes?" Dewey said.

"You sounding me?"

"No, oldest brother," Dewey mock-whined. "But you get most of your loot from your family . . . I mean the keepers. Truth?"

74

"Well, I got other ways."

"But most is from the old folks in prison. Truth?"

"So?" Lunkface asked threateningly.

"So, they pay taxes. That is *taxed* money you get and you have got the right to class-A service. Isn't that the truth? Ask your father. Am I right, Papa Hector?"

Hector appeared to think it over. "He's right."

"I never thought of it that way."

"I wouldn't shit my brother," Dewey said.

Hinton agreed, nodding gravely; Hector turned away and grinned at the Professor instead.

But the train had been standing still for about five minutes and they began to get nervous. Maybe the word was out; the net was spread; *they* were checking all the trains as they came past, hoping to rope all the warriors who had escaped. It had been more than two hours since the rumble on the plain, but they might still be laying in wait all over. Hinton thought, again, that if they took off the insignia and spread around to different parts of the train, they wouldn't be seen or known, but he didn't say it; he didn't want to be put down. The pony-junkies noticed nothing. They were down, and drowned in the lose-gloom, and were getting those empty-pocket, come-down shakes. And these Hard Men, thinking of what might be waiting for them at the next station, considered their position and what to do if . . .

"What's the next stop, Junior? Where are we, man?"

"I'm not sure."

Hector gave The Junior that stare of contempt he'd tried to avoid in the first place. But the train began to inch-inch along again, stopping and starting, knocking them back and forth, rocking them with the other slobs. These Other let themselves be jerked around, loose that way, by the motion of the train, because they didn't care what happened to them. But the Family braced itself on wide-apart feet and fought it because they had pride. Dewey couldn't take his eyes off the Duchess under the

75

map and the way her face looked up and the way she talked with a God-Who-Had-Not-Made-Good-The-Promise. A big woman, wearing a man's checked lumber jacket, with a fat, lumpy face, button eyes and nose, crammed a candy bar into her buttonhole mouth, dropping chocolate slivers on Tomorrow's Post Position. Lunkface couldn't help staring at the simp in the big black hat and he nudged The Junior to look too. That Lunkface didn't know his own strength and The Junior was bugged, but he looked.

The train started. It moved very slowly. They were beginning to pass banks of quick-rigged emergency lights. Workmen were on the track; they stopped working to look up as the train came slowly past. The train edged along two threads of rail slowly so it wouldn't fall. The rest of the tracks had been removed and there was nothing outside but the drop to the street. Huge cranes towered over the sides of the train, swinging girders; there was the din of riveting; welds flared and smoke bellied upward. The workmen's faces looked weird in the quick-shifting lights. No face stayed whole long, the features changing size, dancing. Maliciously, they peered up and pointed and seemed to leer. It made the men nervous. The train screech-crawled into a station; a loud-speaker was already blurring something at them, not making sense yet, but telling them what they had to do. The tone was loud and commanding. What was it saying? Hector wondered if it was some kind of blockade so the cops could get them? Maybe the workers were really plain-clothes men.

The doors opened. The words came in a little more clearly. Something about the track being out for repair. Transfers. Busses to catch. Train travel resumed further down the line, or on another line. The name of the station made no sense to them since they didn't know what station they were on or where *that* stop was. Was there some kind of sign?

The horse-creeps were somnambulating up slowly and beginning to drift to the doors and file out like they expected it, or it didn't matter. If the hardhands were ambushing, all they had to do was screen themselves behind the pony-sleepers till the Family came up, Hector thought. Maybe they should just stay here. But the cops would get them here, too. Or they would have to ride back where they had come from. Dewey's hand went up and he fingered the insignia on his hat; others must have had the same idea because Bimbo also gave Hector the asking look. Hector frowned and Dewey's hand just made adjusting moves as he twisted and straightened out his pin.

They got out of the train. Everyone was heading one way. The crowd was bunched up at the exit, swirling, compressing into a tight mass. The train doors closed behind them and whether they liked it or not, they were trapped. They moved along slowly. The loud-speaker kept giving out orders again and again in impossible-to-understand sentences. They shuffled ahead. People closed in tight behind the Family and they were penned up and being pushed. The sleepers began to get a little nervous and were coming to life. They surged along a little faster.

Far ahead, near the exit—though only Lunkface was tall enough to see clearly what was going on—everyone seemed to go a little crazy. They were all pushing hard there, talking loud as they tried to funnel through two narrow, one-man doors. They weren't excited around the Family yet. Lunkface yelled "Let's get out of here," and the Family tried to phalanx up and spear through. The sleepers still ambled, some of them still calculating on their dream sheets, holding the figures close to their faces under the dim, shaky, platform lights.

At first the Dominators shoved ahead a little faster, keeping tight formation. But the wave of excitement at the exit of the station house began to travel back along the thick line of people. Everyone around the Family became agitated and began to push

77

forward harder. There was no wind; it was very hot here. Everyone wanted to get it over with. Irritated, people began to ask, "What's the holdup?" and "Come on, come on," over and over again. The Family was made more nervous by the chant; they didn't know anything; they weren't making way fast enough; the longer they hung around, the sooner the cops might come down on them.

Then, from the roof tops, on a level with and alongside the station, a line of punky tots stuck their heads above the roof balustrade and began to sound them all up and down, cursing them in Spanish and English making sheep-sounds. The kids made drum and bugle sounds with their mouths and then began to fling lit firecrackers at them, using the overhand grenade-throwing swing. Everyone began to curse them out but, safe across about fifteen feet of four-story drop, the kids gave better than they got. And now, the mob behind the Family, driven by the firecrackers, began to close up and push harder.

The Family was driven around. They shouldered and high-elbowed with Lunkface pointing the wedge. They began to drive through faster, holding on to one another, finding comfort from the feel of one another, merged into a hard oneness among the wild particles of the Other that beat against them. They caught up the Simp, the Professor, and the Duchess in front of them and plowed them along for a few feet. Everyone was beginning to noise it now. The Simp's eyes were wider, more moronic; his hat flopped around his head without falling off and he threw himself all around, grinning more and more as he hit out. The Simp hit into the Professor who was still nibbling on his sandwich which jammed into his face. The Professor began a long speech in a krauty accent, crumbs yelling out of his mouth. The Simp hit against Lunkface who tried to hit back but couldn't swing his hands free. The Dominator drive carried only about four feet and they piled into a solid reef of people, clogged, cackling for no reason at all. Pushed, the Other screamed and laughed angrily. Excitement kept passing along like a wave coming by, up, and behind them and the whole line rammed forward and smashed up against their backs. The Junior, who was in back, tried to turn with Bimbo to face the pressure but, caught sideways, was almost thrown down. Hinton, helpless, was lofted and carried for a moment, his legs dangling, useless. Even Lunkface became scared. As they all got nearer to the doors of the station house, it began to get wilder and wilder.

They were all jammed up in the station house; free hands waved; the roar was deafening. Everyone had to file between the change booth and a railing to get a transfer, unless they just wanted to cut out. But nobody was going to leave without that pass. And now, his hour come round, an old change-booth man, wearing a celluloid eyeshade, his head thrown back, looked down out of the bottoms of his eyes as if considering which of the hands clawing in at him through the space under the grill was worthy, and then doled out transfers with disdainful and deliberate jabs, safe in his cage, impervious to the screaming faces stuck against the grill.

The Simp's face was completely twisted now; a little drool ran down the side of his chin. He had gotten his hand around the Duchess somehow and she was whooping. The stubbled face of the Professor was splayed out and he was saying something which sounded like, "Let us behave like human beings. Let us have a little dignity. Let us have a little reason," while the roar inside the station house beat all around and that calm old man behind the grill, who to show he had control, not only of the situation, but of himself, didn't hear the curses screamed at him, and didn't bother to smile in triumph.

Hector saw that it was almost pointless to try for transfers. They were all crazy; it was too frightening. He yelled for his children to turn off and not to bother with the change booth. But

79

they almost couldn't free themselves. Panicky Lunkface beat a space around himself with his fists and got them out and they were through the turnstiles and past the doors and clattering down the stairs faster and faster, pushing people aside, running away from the roaring scream behind them. An indignant voice said, "God-damned J.D.s."

There was a big line in the street being filtered slowly into the buses which were there to take the passengers to where the trains resumed running. A few soldiers leaned against a candy-store newsstand, laughing at the coolie mob scene. They saw the men come off and from the way their faces immediately chilled, the Family could see that they were alerting: the enemy on their turf. There were only three soldiers, so they didn't make trouble, but one of them took off casually, strolled a few steps, cut fast into the darkness and was out of sight. Hector knew what that meant: reinforcements. The other two stayed edgy, but cool, showing heart.

They didn't know where they were. They didn't know whose country they were in, but they knew they were in trouble. By now every truce in the whole city was off and they had been spotted because they were uniformed and they wore their insignia.

Hector called up The Junior and asked, "Man, where do we go?"

"I don't know."

"You were supposed to be watching the stations."

"I didn't know we'd stop like that."

"Which way do we go?"

"I don't know."

"I'll deal with you later." Hector decided they would move out and follow down along the line of the tracks. They couldn't wait for the bus because they would have to hang around that block-long line with those wild Other. Who knew what would happen before they got away. Soldiers were probably moving up. The thing to do, Hector decided, was to parley for safe passage.

July 5th, 1:30–2:30 A.M.

It was hotter, here in the street. The buildings cut off the air from the sides and the tracks of the elevated closed in above. Firecracker strings were being shot off all around; the noise came down to them from the dark side streets; now and then heavier stuff went off. The two soldiers standing in front of the candy store were looking jazzed-up, wearing pegged pants and bright, striped shirts; their high, cloth-front shoes were held together with pearl buttons; they wore wide-brimmed, straw plantation-owner hats set low over their faces so they had to tilt their heads back to look down on anyone they talked to. You could just tell, Hector thought, they were practically off the plane from the mother-island. Hector hoped they spoke English well enough because he, Bimbo, and Lunkface didn't talk Span-

81

ish too well; they'd been born here and knew better than to wear pegged pants.

"A bunch of Juanny-come-lately *miras*," Hector whispered to his men. The *miras* were giving them the cold look because the Dominator uniforms were raggedy now because they'd been through a hard battle. The *indigenos* gave them the stare—as if to say who were these rag-bag outsiders to come invading their turf without proper permits and parley. They faced each other up and down, but everyone was careful to keep his face grave; Bimbo watched Lunkface to see that he didn't make trouble, but even Lunkface knew enough not to show he had more heart than sense—not here, not now. The Other, on the breadline, didn't notice anything at all, sheeping into the waiting buses.

As they were looking each other over, a girl came out of the candy store and joined the two *miras*. She was wearing a white pleated skirt that hung only halfway between her knees and that promised land, dark stockings, brass-buckled, red-leather shoes, covering her ankles with spiky heels that muscled her calves. She was wearing a short-waisted, sleeveless paradise flowered blouse that left her trim brown waist bare. Her face was painted; her eyes big, rimmed with whorish black stuff, the lips smeared with shiny, white lipstick, eyebrows penciled high into arcs of perpetual amusement, and fluttering big eyelashes, probably fake, Hector thought, because there was make-up crusted on them. Though her skin was brown, her eyes were gray; the Family could feel, almost at once, that stirring, but they took care to keep their faces smooth. Her hair was up in big rollers and loosely covered with a white kerchief titled MEMORIES OF PUERTO RICO.

Hector advanced alone to parley. The smaller of the *miras* pushed himself loose from the wooden newsstand as if it required great effort. A cigarillo dangled from his lips; his thumbs were hooked in his belt, shoulders hunched, elbows crooked a

82

little forward. He ambled up to meet Hector halfway between the Family and the candy store. They looked at each other's uniform and thought the other showed nothing, but they kept grave masks. Hector started to talk; he couldn't afford to play the waiting game to see who lost prestige by starting first. After all, they were in hostile country. Hector explained: they had been forced off the train by the construction; they were going *through* to Brooklyn; there was no matter of dispute here at all. Dominators were coming home from the Big Meeting—everyone knew about Ismael's assembly. They asked permission to march through the turf to the next train, wherever that was, as a peace party. After all, there was a city-wide cool on, wasn't there? Hector didn't say that his men were unarmed.

The other puffed his cigarillo hard and gave Hector the narrow-eyed and steady look while he considered it, his face wise behind the rising smoke. Hector noticed he had long sideburns. The *mira* said, thick-accented, he knew nothing of a city truce; he knew nothing of any Big Meeting of the gangs. If such a thing had happened, why weren't his men, the Borinquen Blazers, invited? Didn't the leaders think that his men had enough *machissmo?* Hector realized he had made a mistake in talking about the meeting. He told the Borinqueno that everyone had heard of the Blazers, but such arrangements hadn't been up to them in the first place, and things turned out wrong in the second place. Behind the little leader, the girl was giving The Dominators the up and down, trying to decide how much men they were. Even though her face, those legs, that flash of bare middle excited Hector, he recognized the old trouble-making look: a bitch.

They parleyed back and forth a little about the safe passage. The little leader said he didn't know if he could let the Family through. After all, the matter should be discussed in council. They talked a little about one another's reps, what brother gangs

83

they ran with, what interborough affiliations they had, who they knew. But though the Dominators and the Blazers had never heard about one another, they took care to admit one another's big reps. They pulled out clippings: Hector's from the *Daily News;* the little leader's from *La Prensa,* in which their gang's raids and bops were written up. They bragged how many men they could field. Hector said that they had a Youth Board Worker. The little Borinqueno had to admit that they didn't have a worker yet, but they were busting out hard and should be assigned one any day now. Hector hastened to say that the Youth Board was overworked, short-handed and it was short-sighted on the Board's part, not so much an insult.

The girl was chewing gum and smoking a cigarette, looking at the diplomats coolly, staring at the Family, turning to talk softly to the other Blazer now and then, swirling as she turned so they could see where the tops of her rolled stockings cut into her thighs. She did a few dance steps. The sound of her heels clicking on the sidewalk made them edgy.

Hector offered a cigarette to the little leader; the Borinqueno took it—a good sign. They compared their individual reps and gave one another full credits as tough warriors. The talkers relaxed a little, but the Family wondered what was taking so long. What if they were being kept here while reinforcements were being brought up? Bimbo coughed twice to warn Hector. The girl went back into the candy store and came out with a Coke. She stuck it into her mouth slowly, her lips low around the neck, tilted the bottle up, a little to the side so she could keep challenging them with that stare. Bimbo watched Lunkface. Lunkface didn't do anything; he was still keeping his head. The little leader decided that there was nothing wrong with the Family taking passage through the territory of the Borinquen Blazers, as long as they came in peace. Hector spread his fingers, palms up. So he told Hector it was a matter of following elevated tracks

84

down two, three stops, he wasn't sure. The buses went there and train service began again.

But the girl was bored. She had been hanging around all day and nothing interesting had happened. Sure, some of the boys had brought a little wine for her. She had gone off and had a little fun with some of them. But the whole day had been dragging and now she was a little headachy because the wine was wearing off. She yawned—it was much too early to go home—was there any fun in shooting off firecrackers? Mankid stuff. The invaders looked interesting, almost men. Now, if she could promote a little excitement for herself, things might look up. She could boast about what her powers were; armies fought over her.

She came up to the little leader, and they all knew they were going to have a little trouble. Hector hoped the little leader had control enough to stay cool. The little leader knew what was happening, too, and he decided that they wouldn't have any trouble; certainly it was pointless. They were outnumbered; reinforcements hadn't come up yet. Maybe Chuchu was having trouble finding everyone at this time of the night, or they were all off having fun with explosives.

The girl looked Hector up and down and turned away a little, raised the Coke bottle, surrounded the glass rim with her lips, clicking it against her teeth. The boldness embarrassed the truce makers, but the little leader didn't have the sense, or the manhood, to stop her. Hector would have just slapped her away. She turned and looked the Family's dirty clothes over in the cool way that always meant "show me." The Blazer who thought he had control got irritated without knowing why. Hector turned his face away carefully and looked back at the Family. No one was moving, not even Lunkface.

The little leader told the Family to hurry up, go, rushing them; he warned them that they would have to cross a thin, block-wide

85

stretch of territory they were warring over with the Castro Stompers, move on to Borinquen territory again, but look out for the Jackson Street Masai on two blocks before they got back on the train.

They were about to leave but the girl said, pointing to Hector's hat, "Where did you get that pin?"

Hector said that he had made it.

She said that she would like one.

Hector said that they only had one Sign apiece.

"What does it mean?"

"It's the mark of our Family."

"I never saw one like it. I'd like one."

"We don't have any extra."

"Give me yours."

"I can't. That's the insignia of our men. I'm the leader."

"Then take one from your men."

"Bitch, stop making trouble," the little leader said.

"I'm not making trouble. But look, man, are you going to let them parade through our land wearing insignia? It's an insult."

"You just want one. Stop making trouble."

"I'm not making trouble. But what if the word gets around you let some army walk through our land at will? How are you going to look then? What are the others going to think about it? Soon, the Stompers and the Masai, they are going to mambo in, man."

"You just want one for yourself."

The bitch smiled, stamped her heels, twisted her white skirt till it whirled up above her stocking tops again. "Some man you are."

"All right," the little leader said. "Stop egging me."

"You're the chicken; I egg," and she put her lips around the bottle again, pushing out her cheek two or three times. She looked at the Family from under her long, black lashes.

86

The little leader made a motion to backhand her; she stuck her face close, bottle under, holding her jaw up for him to slam but he didn't hit her. Any Dominator would have creamed her.

"All right," the little leader said; "I'm not going to fall for your jazz, and you're not going to get the pin. But I'll show you Jesus Mendez is no chicken. You," he told Hector. "You just take them pins off and you can passage through this homeland with no trouble at all. We'll even give you an escort. But you can't army through."

"The pins are our mark. They don't mean we're at war. They just tell you who we are."

"You go through as civilians—all right. You go through as soldiers—no good. We come down on you. You take them pins off. We don't want them, but she's right. You can't trample our territory without showing respect."

"You're going to let her make your policy for you, man?"

And the little leader got angrier; it was hot, he didn't want to spend the whole night talking, he was nervous because help wasn't marching up. "Listen, no woman runs this army. The Borinquen Blazers are all men and all strong and we have a lot of rumbles to our credit—you can ask anyone around here. But how is it going to look to the enemy if we let you march through here? We'd be put down, laughed at, and warred on."

Hinton thought that it might be a good idea to take off the pins; so did Dewey. They didn't say anything.

But the little leader's attitude was annoying; the way the bitch kept posturing, shaking her ass, showed that she was running the play here, but Hector didn't dare do anything about it. If the Family had her alone for a while, they would show her what the score was. They stood there in the heat. Above, the train started to back out of the station, rumbling back uptown. They didn't say anything till it got quieter. Firecrackers were still going off up the sidestreets. Well, it was simple, Hector thought: just waste the little leader a little, take off, take the slut with them—that might do it. But who knew what she had around her. Maybe—and she looked like just the girl to do it—she was packed for her boy—a blade between her tits, a gun strapped between her legs.

Hector said, "Well, fuck you, man. We're not coolies. We're warriors. We're going through. We're going through in peace, remember that, man, but the Coney Island Dominators is one Family that moves with its signs. I mean we don't punk out because some shake-ass woman . . ."

The little leader turned his back on Hector and went back to the candy store. Hector saw it was time to move out. "Remember, we're moving in peace," he called.

"Good-looking," the bitch told Hector; "Why don't you give me that pin and I'll make it all right for you."

"Fuck yourself," he told her.

"Don't talk to me like I was a whore. Man, I'll show you who'll get fucked, you motherfucker."

Hector turned around and waved the Family into the quick-march downtown, along the route of the elevated tracks. They walked a block, crossed the street and started down the next one when they saw that the other Blazer and the girl were following the Family. Hector ordered them to quicken the pace. They were getting scared. They walked a half-block and Hector held up his hand and they all stopped. The trailer and the bitch stopped too, moved back against the store front and waited. The Family jittered. They pulled at their clothing. They kept plucking their pants free from between their sweating buttocks and away from their crotches. They were getting frightened now, moving restlessly, impatient, ready to cut out and start running downtown.

"All right, sons," Hector told them; "If that is the way they are going to have it, then we are going to move out like a war party, and if they come up on us, why we'll burn them and lay them waste."

"Man, I wish I had artillery," The Junior said.

"Don't dream," Hector said. "We wanted peace. You all know we wanted peace."

They said, "Yes."

"But they wouldn't let us be."

"No," they all said.

"They never let us alone. Always after us. Man can't breathe."

They all said "No." They were beginning to get angry.

"We tried. We tried. Never leave you alone."

"No peace," they said.

"Bimbo!"

Bimbo, the bearer, came up. He knew what was wanted. He took a red cigarette case out of his pocket. The soft, cardboard-backed leather was crusted with colored little cut-glass-headed tacks, gleaming like diamonds. He opened it. Inside were black-paper cigarettes with white tips. They moved close. Bimbo tapped six cigarettes out and gave them to Hector. Hector put one in his mouth; Bimbo lit it; Hector inhaled deeply, held it, and exhaled and they all said "aaaah." Hector pinched out the tip. They watched him carefully; he didn't flinch. They nodded. Hector put the butt, white tip up, into his hat band. Bimbo gave him the second whiskey-bottle, and Hector drank. Then Hector stuck the other five cigarettes into his mouth and Bimbo lit them all. Hector gave four back to Bimbo. He puffed the fifth ciga-rette. Bimbo genuflected in front of Hector, took the cigarette from him, said, "This brother will serve his Family till he dies," pinched out the coal and stuck the sign in the side of his hat band, and also took a drink.

Lunkface, whose sense of tradition was at war with his pa-tience said, "Hurry that up, man, they'll be coming down on us."

But they all gave Lunkface the cold look because this was the important moment. Bimbo took the third cigarette, puffed it, and tapped Lunkface. Lunkface kneeled in front of Bimbo and Bimbo gave Lunkface his cigarette to puff. Lunkface said the words, stuck the snuffed-out cigarette behind his ear, and took his drink. They were beginning to feel a little better now, getting tight and cool, their fear growing into anger, and they began to bounce a little on the balls of their feet, working themselves up.

The other sons went through it, sticking the cigarettes into the backs of their hats. As each man said that this brother would serve his Family till he died, they felt, more and more, the fighting spirit uniting them into one, till they could take on anyone; feeling drunk with it, drawing closer, closer, Father, Uncle, brother-children, all together tight, because they had all sucked from one another's lips, were one, gang-person-family, blood-united, ready and able to stand up to any fucking Other in the whole fucking world. Hector, speaking loud, chanting angry; "I mean we come down here and we want peace and we're not no Commies jiving sounding putting down anyone of them and they come on like they have to have war because of that slut."

They all said "Yes."

"Well, now we move out like a war party, even though we wanted peace. Anyone could tell you we wanted peace. Well, now it's too late for that."

"Yah! We wanted peace," they shouted.

The bottle was finished. Bimbo flung it far into the air toward where the trailer and the bitch skulked. It arched and shone high, but splintered short of the mark; the bitch and the Blazer bounced high over the fragments slivering along the sidewalk.

Now they moved out, swiftly, leader and brothers, all knowing exactly what to do, bonded into One. Muscle tightened, compressing body a little so that biceps bunched, and triceps tensed, fist balled, shoulder hunched, legs flexed, trunk tilting, every part taut to sense.

The Family considered going down one of the side streets and moving parallel to the main street till they came to the station. But the side streets were smaller. If the Borinquens had a tank to bring up, they could come blazing down on the Family, catch them, and who knew if there would be doorways to dive into? If they were japped from the roofs with Molotov cocktails here, it was a matter of deploying into the middle of the street, under the elevated tracks where they would be shielded. A scout, The Junior, moved out at a trot till he was a block ahead. No one told him to; he knew. Hinton dropped back about a block to bring up the rear. Scout and Rear stayed on opposite sides of the street so they could command more space as the eyes of the war party. The slut and the trailer followed. They could see her white skirt in the dimness, moving in and out of the street lights. A string of small-arms firecrackers fired off to their left; they startled; head ducked down and around, heart pounded faster, sweat beaded out in sudden spurts.

A soft, hot wind sprang up in front of them, opposing them with a stream of damp air. They leaned forward. The Family eye kept busy searching for anything to form weapons fast in case of a jap. If the attacking army came in a tank, or outnumbered them, the Family might make it to a fire-alarm box and pull the lever; cops and firemen would come and they could be saved; but that was the extreme thing to do. They kept alert for the orange lights that showed where the alarm boxes were.

The Family saw cars—good—car antennas to break off for flails. Garbage cans were everywhere—covers good for shields. It was pointless to run. Who knew how far they would have to run, and they couldn't lose face under the enemy fire. The point spotted nothing suspicious ahead; the rear signaled that they were still being trailed. The Family sweated now; the moving air

91

was getting stickier; the closeness of the air smelled of a near enemy. The wind was gusting dust and papers into their faces. Tension was beginning to strain their muscles. Every time a car drove by, someone jumped and they looked carefully to see how old the man driving it was. They watched every passerby, but there were very few of these and they wished the streets were crowded.

They passed an apartment building. A lot of broken furniture was lying around in the street. It worried the family. Might mean an assembly and ammunition dump: tables with legs fixed to come off easily, couch springs for wire whips, guns stashed away in the fluffy arms of busted-down easy chairs, ash-can covers for shields and ash cans full of broken Coke bottles to fling, rocks, used light bulbs, pipe ends, loosened spikes in the iron fence, old-fashioned spear-headed cast-iron floor lamps, stacked bricks, and oiled excelsior bunches to fire and fling from the rooftops. All the enemy had to do was to boil out of the doorways, race up from behind the stoops and the whole arsenal—nothing the cops could call weapons—was ready for them. The Family would have to run a gauntlet under the fort. But the houses were very old here, and there was a reason for throwing out furniture, and a street this wide was never a good place to ambush anyone. It couldn't be blocked off from the ends; it couldn't really be controlled from the roofs and, for that matter, the cops could easily come down on everyone with their superior tank force, cordon off the whole battlefield and take both sides in.

Lunkface broke formation and ran over to the pile and started to tear loose a table leg.

Hector told him to drop it and remember they still moved in peace. "Give them Blazers no cause."

"Well, man, you're not going to trust them to care about that, are you?" Lunkface asked.

"The Family makes no move yet."

The Family sense was better attuned to this land now. They

92

were not jumpy, only battle tense, sorting the sounds into innocent and dangerous. The wind bugged them. They came to the
Freeman Street station, but it was blocked off and they went on.
Hinton had lived around here once, but it didn't look familiar
anymore. The Family hoped the territory of the Borinquen Blazers would end here, but the chalked wall-signs told them they
were still deep in enemy country. A bus passed them packed full
of track-loonies from the train. Lunkface pointed and they saw
the Professor standing there; he looked like he was still making
his speech to no listeners.

Hector had an idea. If they could only capture the Blazer,
they could hold him as a hostage. Or better, they would let him
go and that would show the Borinquenos that their intentions
were honorable. They wouldn't even touch the slut. Whatever
they did to her, no matter how innocent, that bitch was going to
say that they had fingered her and insulted her and spit on the
honor of the Blazers. But they couldn't stop to jap the right way
because they had to keep moving at a raid pace, keeping alert
for any party coming down on them. How could they trap the
trailer here? Hector wondered. If they moved into the next land,
they could alter their strategy and spring the snare right. But
where were the borders?

They passed undershirted men seated in front of an apartment
house. There were tots still playing in the street. The men had
brought out chairs and boxes and set up a bridge table. A wire
from a ground-floor apartment was strung out and two lamps lit
a too-hot-to-sleep card game. A baby was sleeping in a carriage;
one of the players rocked with one hand and held his cards with
the other. The men froze their play and looked the Family over,
carefully without staring insultingly, as they passed. The radio
played *pachanga* music to keep the card game gay: drums, bon-
goes, and cowbells echoed down the very still street. As they
passed they heard the players begin to talk.

They waited for the attack as they moved; the tension became acute again; the muscle ached; the senses dulled with the strain of being at attention too long, and they probed harder into the dangerous night. The wind died down. The dust settled. It seemed stiller. There were fewer explosions. The air became almost palpable; the sweat was drenching their shirts to their jackets again. And now, as they passed another shut-down station, the sounds they had learned to interpret as nonhostile began to become suspicious again. An explosion like the smash and thud of a Molotov cocktail breaking into flame jumped them. Somebody with a grease gun was beginning to spray them and Dewey started to throw himself prone when he realized it was a string of firecrackers rattling off. Not being packed for any action, not even having one knife among them, they worried that they wouldn't be able to get hold of any defensive weapon on time to fight back if they came. Or if they came down in a car—everything would be lost. The way the lead's head was turning, in sudden jerks, meant he was alarmed at everything. If he broke and ran, they would all panic. Hector had to get them out of it. He didn't know how much further they had to go. Mysterious open windows, black, looked down on them from the apartment houses. A sniper would lurk in any one of those windows, ready to pick them off. It was not like being on a raid in traditional rivals' territory—territory that was as well scouted as their own, where they knew a lot of ways to get home, and when they did there were a million covers to be safe in if there was a chase. Where could they go now?

Then Hector came up with the plan. He gave Bimbo, Lunkface, and Dewey the word. Bimbo faded back to tell Hinton. At the same time Dewey ran down and gave the action to The Junior. The girl's white skirt still swirled behind; if the trailer had any idea of giving it up and cutting out, that cunt was going to keep him going to make up for her honor; she was going to get a pin tonight, Hector thought. Bimbo and Dewey came back.

The Junior increased his pace to double time. Hector, Bimbo, Lunkface, and Dewey quick-marched. But Hinton slowed up just a little. They began to draw out of sight of their trailers. It helped when the tracks turned a corner and the train route left Southern Boulevard and kept on going down along Westchester Avenue. As soon as they were around the corner, the men fanned out and holed into store doorways. Then Hinton passed and caught up with the slowing-up Junior. A few minutes later, the bitch and the Blazer followed along. When they passed the ambushing men, The Junior and Hinton turned and began to charge the tailers who turned and began to run away, as the four Dominators rose out of ambush, surrounded, caught, and held them. The trailer knew enough to stand still but the girl threw herself around, cursed them and shouted for them to get their hands off while Dewey said, laughing, showing his teeth very big, World War II Jap style, "Ah ssso, Captain Sssstrongheart. You are sssurprissed?"

The girl began to noise it loud when Lunkface, who had her, clapped his big hand over her mouth.

Hector told her, "You keep raising your voice and we'll give you something to raise it about. Stand still in front of this Family, you hear?" And she stopped fighting.

And then Hector told them he didn't want any war. Did they understand that? And the bitch said that they didn't need any war; why didn't they just give her one of the pins? The trailer told her to shut up and she called him stupid because he had let himself be japped in this simple-minded way. Hector tried to explain it again and asked them if they were going to take back the word to the others that they passed in peace, or was the Family going to have to take them along as hostages, for safety? Lunkface wanted to take the Borinqueno's hat away, but Hector wouldn't let him. The trailer said that as far as he was concerned, they could move in peace: he would bring back the word. The girl said what kind of man was he to surrender to these hick warriors from the hills of somewhere else? The trailer should ask for a fair one right here and now. The trailer told her to shut up because she was going to get him wasted if she didn't shut her big bitch mouth. And while she didn't raise her voice, she kept sounding them all and telling them what nowhere characters they were—halfmen—and if they wanted to get home in one piece, all they had to do was to let her go and to give her one of the pins.

The Family gave her the big laugh and wished they had the time to show her what they did with big-mouth sluts and she was asking for it, but good. Still—and they had known some good ones in their time—they had to admit that she wasn't frightened of them—not one bit—and they had to admit that she had heart, more than the trailer who stayed quiet. They frisked the trailer and found that he had a blade, and they took that away. Spoils of war. They wanted to frisk her too, but they saw the look on the trailer's face. There was no point in making any more trouble than necessary. They wanted to question the trailer—how many soldiers were coming down on them; were there tanks; which way would they come from? But the trailer called on the honor of his band and wouldn't say anything at all. He looked the Family up and down in the cold and Spanish way, angering them. The only thing to do was to teach him with a few lesson-slashes with his own knife. But it was pointless to do so.

And in the meantime, the bitch kept lipping them, one and all, and mostly the trailer. What was he supposed to do, Bimbo wondered? She called him a one-ball, half-cock, stupid man, and it wasn't the heat he was sweating from, but the hate; he was going to give her that one good, but very good beating when he got her back, for making him out such a fool in the eyes of the grinning Family. The Family had contempt for these Borinquenos; none of them could control their women one shit-worth.

96

And then Bimbo had the thought: "what if they were putting on an act to keep them there. It was time to pull out and march on down the line and get out of this hot and dangerous country. Bimbo signaled speed-up warnings. Hector gave the sign to the prisoner-holders, and they let go of the trailer. Hector said, "On your way, *amigo,* and say only that we march in peace." The Junior moved out to take his point position. The bitch sounded them and the trailer started to pull her away, but she swung free, slapped him, and lunged back for Lunkface's pin. Lunkface leaned away a little and she missed.

The Family started to move out, Hinton lingering to be the Rear, when Lunkface said, "If you want that pin so bad, chick, just come along with us. I mean we're the men. I mean we, you know, ball the best, and we're the biggest men in this whole wide city. Everyone knows the Dominators. I mean you'll be like a sister to us, you know?"

And that was the wrong thing to say because the trailer gave them a look that, under other circumstances, might have cost him a slash or two, a gun-burning, a chain across the face. Even cautious Bimbo wanted to wipe that irritating Spanish Pride off his face, but Hector held him back.

"You," he told the bitch, "move off."

The bitch didn't move. She grinned at Hector and said, "What's the matter, Chico, you don't think you're enough *hombre* for me?"

But Hector was cool and used to being sounded, so he didn't bother to answer her. He waved his arm and the men began to move out.

"You'll give me your pin?" the bitch asked Lunkface. He said he would. She told them that she would go with them. The trailer warned the bitch that she would get what was coming to her. And she said that she didn't know if she was even going to come back to this land of the cuckoos and the capons, and followed the Family. They moved for a block, easier now, faster, but after a while the word was flashed that the trailer was still behind them and they tensed up again. The bitch said not to worry because the Blazers weren't out in force tonight. Most of the men were busy shooting off those kid-stuff fireworks somewhere or other, scattered, and she doubted if they could muster more than five or six men. And anyway, they would soon be over the border.

They passed walls on which the contending Castro Stompers and Borinquen Blazers insulted one another in multi-colored chalks, while the Intervale Avenue Lesbos said they sucked and had more manhood than any little-boy.

After two more Borinqueno blocks, they crossed into a new country. The bitch said there was a truce between the Borinquens and the Jackson Street Masai. Soon they would be coming to the station where they could take the train out.

"Don't let these Masai coons funk you, because the Blazers have them in control," she said. Dewey looked angrily at her.

Lunkface told the girl again that she could be a sister to them and she gave him a look. But he explained what being a sister was and she grinned and said she would, brother, so long as he gave her the pin to show her he really loved her like a sister. They laughed at that. Hector only hoped she wasn't going with them to bring down the others.

They were almost out of it, but muscle couldn't untense; body remained crouched; fist clenched; moving through the heat, wanting to knock and smash at anything, to let it out, loosen, because there had been no fight. Bimbo felt the girl looking at him and hammered the side of his fist against a sign. Her little smile rewarded him. But Lunkface, jealous, strutted stiffly, looking to hit something bigger, to let out the choked spasm. To show her, to live up to her spunkiness. The Junior kept turning back to look at her; Hinton rear-guarded too close. Dewey sulked apart, still angry. Hector watched: A woman on a raid was always trouble. Trust Lunkface to initiate it. Did she give him a wink? Lunkface frowned at Hector and pulled her closer. There was nothing to do but to get rid of her as soon as they could. Hector angrily signaled The Junior and Hinton to watch carefully. He didn't know how he was going to pry her away, because Lunkface was going to fight for the snatch. Maybe just leave the two of them.

They saw the next station a few blocks ahead—the station from which they could get the train home. A man looked them over for a second as he passed. Lunkface, whose arm was around the bitch's neck left her and walked over to the man, caught his arm, turned him around and said, "What you looking at?"

The man said, "Get your hands off me, you snotty punk." He looked big, thick-necked, like he used his hands for a living and had his fight or two.

"Why you look at my sister that way?" Lunkface wanted to know. He had moved in front of the man. The others, excited by the talk, were moving up around the man.

"Are you studs going to let that coolie insult my honor?" the girl said. Hinton was moving up and The Junior was coming back from the point.

"You punks think you own the street. Out of my way."

"Who're you talking to like that?" Hector asked.

And then the man moved fast, trying to break through. He swung at Lunkface. Lunkface, hit on the chest, staggered back. Someone yelled. They were on the man, hitting at him. He tried to back up to the wall, but they were around him. Bimbo had out the first empty whiskey bottle and swung down for the man's head; he missed, hit his wrist on the man's head, and the bottle shot out of his hand and shattered on the floor; someone kicked Bimbo in the shins. They punched the man down and began

99

kicking at him. The bitch danced around them, "Go. Go. Go, go. Gogogo," voicing up to a shriek, reaching through to all of them, the scream-note exciting them. They were standing away from the man now, kicking at him, stomping at his arms and legs. The man tried to move away; it infuriated them and they kicked harder at the sides, stomach, legs; the man lay still, it maddened them and they bent down to punch at his stomach, face, groin. The man turned over—his polo-shirt was bloody from the glass. They kicked his head and beat at his shoulders, his back, wherever they could get at him, and he rolled over again onto his back. And the girl's voice rose higher and higher till it was a throbbing scream and she was hopping up and down, and then the Borinqueno's knife was in Bimbo's hand. Lunkface and Dewey stomped on the man's hands and held them to the floor. Bimbo thrust down. The man screamed; the body jerked violently; the feet on the hands held the body in place; his scream drove them all a little wilder. Bimbo drew out the knife and the man rolled his head back and forth. The face was bloody from the glass; the nose was broken; his mouth was bleeding. Bimbo yelled "Catch," and threw the knife into the air, point downward. It hovered. Lunkface's hand went out to catch it by the handle and, continuing the fall, thrust it down; the man moved a little and the blade went into his side, to the right of the heart, and the bitch screamed again. Her eyes were half-closed and her mouth was open wide and she panted between shrieks and circled and pushed at the Family yelling, "Me. Me. Me. Give it to me. Me too. Me." And Lunkface, pulling out, threw the knife up into the air and Hector caught it and shot it downward, coolly, ripping into the man's face, and skin flapped loose from the sliced-apart cheek. The bitch screamed and Hector drew the knife out and hefted it higher into the air, and this time The Junior caught it and slashed down and caught the man as he tried to roll free from the feet standing on his

100

hands. The Junior got him in the hip and threw the knife up as the bitch followed the way it flew up and saw the faint lights from the street lamps gleaming along its blade and blood, tried to leap up, reaching among the men to catch it herself, but they were too close together. This time Dewey caught it and plunged it down and caught the man in the heart and the man moaned and the moan was long and drawn-out and excited them more because it lingered. The girl was saying, "Give me the knife, give me the knife." But Dewey threw it into the air and yelled, "Your service," to Hinton, and Hinton caught, took, and slashed the knife down into the body.

The bitch was leaning against the wall, her legs spread wide for balance, her belly heaving, her eyes glazed, her open mouth fixed in a grin, panting.

Lunkface said, "Man, look at this sister." And he took her and started to put her down on the floor.

She said, weakly, "No. It's enough. I've had it, man."

Lunkface, holding her shoulders, kicked out her legs and had her down and hitched up her skirt, pulled off her pants and was pushing inside her quick while she said softly, "No, man. Enough, I told you. Enough."

The men circled them and put their arms around one another's necks, looked down, and began to stamp their feet for rhythm.

She rolled and rolled and kept saying that she'd had enough, but she was beginning to enjoy it as they slowly began to increase the stamp-tempo. Lunkface finished quickly, stood up, and they went one after the other, while the others stood around and continued to step up the stamp beat.

Hinton was the last to go on her and by now her face was completely rigid and her eyes saw nothing at all and she was almost unconscious with the joy of it—this big kick—and Hinton looked at her face and was almost frightened because she

101

was something else—mad. Hinton picked up the rhythm of the rabbiting beat, but he almost felt nothing, pumping wildly to keep up with their stampstampstamp. But since nothing was happening, he pretended that he came and jerked out and got to his feet and they were all ready to move out.

Bimbo the bearer kneeled over her, put his hand under her stocking roll and wiped the blade between his thumb and forefinger.

They cut out, running, and left the girl behind. They ran a block to the station and ran up the stairs. Bimbo put tokens in the turnstile for all of them and asked the directions. The cashier told them about how to change to the Coney Island train at 42nd Street. They could see the cashier giving the Family a cautious look, like he expected to get held up. They walked out on the platform. There was no train waiting. They walked to the back end of the platform and looked down. Under the dim street lights, they could see the body lying there. They could see the white skirt and the naked hips, belly, and thighs; she was still there, her head still pillowed on the body.

Elbows on the railing, they watched. She didn't move for about five minutes. And then she turned over. Slowly, she got to her feet and staggered a little. She stood there for a second—patted her skirt, and began to say something. At first they couldn't make out the words; then they heard her, faintly. She was cursing them out, the words becoming clearer and clearer. She shook her fist toward downtown. Her hand dropped. She stopped yelling. She turned slowly, lurched, caught herself, and walked away, standing straighter, going faster and faster back along the way she had come.

"Man," Lunkface said. "We should have taken her with us. She was fun."

July 5th, 2:30—3:00 A.M.

They were leaning against a railing, under the station lamps, waiting for the train to come. They slouched looser and looser, bent easy, tired now. Their faces were empty, staring; Lunkface's mouth was open and his eyes half-shut. He yawned.

Hector said, "Now they know the kind of men we are. No one steps on the Dominators," and he yawned.

Lunkface said, "I still think we should have taken the bitch along."

"But man, she was a slut. I mean any girl who would do it that way . . . Them women; only blood satisfies them," and Bimbo smiled. The Junior giggled.

Dewey started to yawn but his yawn broke into a soft, hysterical laugh. He couldn't stop and the Junior began to laugh and

103

Lunkface joined. Soon they were laughing and laughing, tears rolling. Hinton had to sit down on the floor, weak. The laughing died down; someone started it again. After a long while it slowly stopped because they were too weak to laugh.

"She's going to get it when she gets back. They're really going to scar her up," Dewey said.

"Man, I wouldn't worry about that one," Hector said. "Not one little bit. She got it coming to her, but good."

"Yeah. Man, with the brass heart she has, I'll bet you she has them eating out of her hand in no time. Don't worry, that one, she takes care of herself. Still, she was fun," Lunkface said.

"Well man," Dewey laughed again. "Like how would you know, man? I mean, she didn't even know you were in there."

"She let out some scream when I took her. She knew who was up there," Lunkface said.

"No, man, that was The Junior who made her scream, not you. Am I right, Junior? Am I right?"

The Junior giggled.

"You saying I'm not a man, little brother?" Lunkface asked.

"Now did I say that?"

"He didn't say that, Lunkface."

"I heard what he said. And any time he thinks I'm not the man, why there's ways of proving it, you know what I mean?" Lunkface was scowling.

"No need to flip; this little brother, he's only talking."

"Mad? Who's mad? I just don't like being sounded."

"Sounded? Who's sounding? It's just that I heard her . . ." but he didn't finish when he saw Hector's sign to cool it.

But Lunkface was angry now. "I'll show you who's a man," he said and he unzipped his fly. "You bigger than that, man? Who's bigger than that?"

And Dewey let an expression of disgust at Lunkface's utter stupidity cross his face. "Man, that's not the way you show who's the best man. Size don't mean a thing; everyone knows that."

"What do you mean, size don't count? How else?"

"It's the way of the lay, not the size of the prize. Am I right, Junior? Isn't that right, Hinton? I mean there's other ways of telling. Everyone know that. Uncle Bimbo, I ask you, is it size?"

Bimbo, not wanting to get involved, shrugged and said, "I don't know. I know I like it. That's what counts, man. I like it. My woman, she likes it. We like it. Size, that's someone else's worry, not mine, man. She likes it and she lets me know. That makes me Man."

"No, but I'm talking for the sake of argument. Size don't mean a thing. Not one little thing."

"Well, you so smart and you're talking so big. Is yours this big? Is it?" Lunkface shouted.

"I told you."

"Well, what is it?"

"There's ways of telling."

"How? Just you show me how."

"Well, we don't have a woman. That's one way. Another way is to piss the farthest. That's always a sure sign."

"Any time, man. Any time. Right now." Lunkface walked over to the edge of the platform and pissed. The line of urine curved up and reached as far as the outer rail. "All right, wise man, just you beat *that*."

"Well now, I don't know as I have to go. You know, I mean, you are committing a public nuisance. You know that, man? I mean the cops, they are going to come and they are going to take you and put you in the no-stir. Yes sir. And you are going to have the leisure to piss all you want to. Especially when they bang *your* club with *their* club."

"Man, you were lipping me and you're going to back your words or else you deal with me."

And so they had a contest. Except for Lunkface, they all lined up at the platform edge and they pissed over the tracks. Hinton won, going just a little farther, hitting the third-rail guard. Lunkface disputed it because, he claimed, Hinton had his toes over the edge.

More people were coming onto the platform. They kept away from the Family, staying down at the other end. They were afraid of these Brothers, which made the men swagger a little. Hector got tired of the argument and he sent Bimbo to buy candy for them; he was beginning to get hungry. Bimbo came back with six bars. Hector put them into the pocket of his jacket.

"Man, they'll melt there," Dewey said. Hector paid him no mind.

The argument over, they leaned on the rail for a little while. They were even too tired now to worry if the cops were going to come, or if that bitch was going to bring back her gang. Dewey had to sit down on the floor; his jacket was split in the back. They watched the platform filling up and couldn't stop yawning. Dewey almost fell asleep. They tried to work up a little interest in sounding one another, but no one had the energy. After about fifteen minutes, a train came crawling into the station. A mob of passengers went through the same bit that had happened on the other station, but they were orderly about it. The men slouched onto the train and found seats. Five of them sat on one side of the aisle; Hector sat on the other side, facing them.

They sat and yawned and waited; the train wouldn't move. They complained to one another about it. The Junior took out his comic book and started to read. The Junior didn't follow the words too well unless they were printed big, or dark. But he could follow the whole action from the pictures. It was about ancient soldiers, Greeks, heroes who had to fight their way home through many obstacles, but in the end they made it. He had enjoyed reading it so much that it was the third time he was going through.

It was hot in the train and smelled of burned insulation. Some of the fans were broken. No wind blew through the windows. Outside, over the rooftops, the celebration flashes were coming less and less frequently.

Hector took one of the candy bars out of his pocket. They looked expectantly at him, all except The Junior who was bent over his comic book. Dewey clowned it a little, clapped his hands together and made seal noises. Lunkface sat still, his arms folded on his chest; it was coming to him. Two or three passengers sitting at the other end of the train stared apprehensively at them, not sure if they were fooling around or were dangerous. The men made certain that the looks weren't put-down or evil-eye in any way. After all, they were men with a rep and had done big things, especially tonight, and it gave the Family a sense of pride to know they were being looked at with respect.

Hector ate the first bar of candy himself. Their looks pleaded; Dewey made the tongue-hanging face. Hector chewed very slowly to show them who was Father. He reached into his pocket and took out the second bar; it was melty. He held it up. They looked at the candy. He grinned. The Junior concentrated on his comic book. Hector milked it for what it was worth. Lunkface's eyes were empty as he looked dreamily at the bar, picking his nose steadily, deeply, with a thick forefinger, not seeing the bar, remembering the girl. Bimbo nudged Lunkface to pay more attention. Hector stuck his finger under the end of the white, inner wrapping of the chocolate and pushed the bar slowly up through its outer wrapping. They grinned and laughed while Hector simpered, making like a fag. Dewey took him up on it, stood and pranced by, his hands on his hips, pretending that he was fruit and that the candy was the big come-on. Dewey reached out for the candy bar and Hector kept it out of his reach, slapping Dewey's wrist. Dewey became fruitier, begging for it, dog-panting while they nudged one another and laughed. Even The Junior had to look up from a panel showing the grinning faces of the Greek heroes as they saw The Sea. The Sea.

Dewey looked over Hector's head, pretending he saw fireworks: he shouted, "Man, look at that rocket go." Hector turned. Dewey slid the candy up from the outer wrapper, jumped back to his seat, simpering, and hid the candy behind his back. When Hector turned around and saw what had happened, they all pointed him and laughed; Dewey stamped his boot and slapped his thigh. Hector had to laugh too, but they could see it made him angry so Dewey gave back the prize.

Hector peeled back the white wrapping from the chocolate bar; they all leaned across the aisle. Hector joked, yelling, "This is called the circumcision," and that broke them up again. Hector broke off a piece of chocolate and made as if to eat it himself. They all groaned. He looked at Lunkface, but tossed the piece to Bimbo. Bimbo caught it without moving, calmly opening his hand, letting it fall into his grab. They murmured approval. Hector broke off another piece and tossed it, looking in Hinton's direction, to Lunkface. Lunkface tried to catch it fancy, bobbled it, leaving his seat to hold it; someone laughed at his clumsiness. Lunkface turned quickly and they all looked back at him with bland faces. Hector, who knew the laugher, grinned.

The train doors closed. The next piece was for Dewey. It flew through the air. The train jerked, and began to move ahead very slowly. The candy fell in the fold of the comic book and slid to the floor. They all laughed. Hinton picked up the piece of chocolate quickly, handling it as if it were something contaminated, and tossed it up into the air lightly, in Dewey's direction. Dewey shrieked, and shrunk back and batted it lightly to his left. The piece flew in Bimbo's direction; Bimbo jumped out of his seat as if a dirty bug was flying in his direction. The chocolate flew past Dewey toward Lunkface who made clumsy, frantic brushing motions, missing the piece. It hit Lunkface and he tried to get away from it as if it was alive; it fell to the floor again. Lunkface reached into his pocket for his handkerchief to wipe himself, forgetting it was tied around his head with the Family pin on it. He made brushing motions; he reached over and tore a piece of The Junior's comic book and wiped the invisible stain from his fingers. He paid no attention to The Junior's angry yell.

But Hinton kicked the piece of chocolate back in Lunkface's direction. Lunkface jumped high and away. Hinton went and got the crumpled piece of comic-book paper, smoothed it out; it was the panel showing the heroes arriving at the sea. He bent down, picked up the piece of chocolate with the paper and went over to Lunkface, bearing it carefully with both hands, bowed and presented it, his head almost, but not quite, touching the piece of candy.

Lunkface leaned away. "Get that out of here," he told Hinton.

Hinton said, "But why, oh older brother? Keep our city clean. Man, take." And he pushed the candy a little further in Lunkface's direction. Lunkface drew back more. The Junior was smiling, but kept his head straight watching the play out of the corner of his eye. You had to be careful the way you smiled at Lunkface.

Lunkface said, "Get that thing out of here, man, get it away."

"But it's from Dewey. That Dewey, your younger brother, he offers it. It's from Dewey."

"You get that thing away from me. Man, get it away. I'll burn you. I'll waste you. Watch yourself."

Hinton turned around to Hector. Hector stopped grinning and looked serious. Some of the other people in the car were smiling in their direction; Hector decided that there was nothing de-

109

meaning in the smiles. "He won't take it, Papa. Make him take it, Papa," Hinton shouted.

"He won't take it," Hector shouted back and shrugged his shoulders.

Dewey came up beside Hinton, bent down and peered at the candy. He said, "Dust. A few hairs, man. A little soot. Some snot. Only some spit. You look," he said and took it and passed it to The Junior, laying it on his comic book.

The Junior took great care not to touch the candy. He brought it close to his face, peered, and said, "It's not so dirty," to Dewey. "It's not so dirty, Lunkface," he yelled.

"Don't go jiving me. Don't go putting me down," and Lunkface's fists were closed; he looked in Hector's direction. Hector made sure his mouth was closed, his face was serious, and that he was judging the whole thing impartially. The train crawled down into the tunnel; the heat closed around them; the wind that was blown in from the windows was hotter, damp, carrying strange smells and sounds. The stink of burning insulation permeated everything, irritating their noses, watering their eyes. The fan wheezed and beat against the air, stirring floor dust from the aisles. The train stopped; more people got on. They gave the Family *that* look, as if they recognized what they had to deal with and tried to keep in the other part of the car. Because they knew they were being watched, they acted it a little wilder, pretending there was no one else in the world. The doors closed. The train tried to start, made a few jerks and stood still, the motor vibrating under their feet. They began to worry a little that they might have to go through that change-over again. Finally the train moved out and they turned their attention back to the candy comedy.

Hinton held the paper with the candy out; Lunkface knocked it aside. Dewey said, "Man, you're littering. That is a crime, you hear now; a misdemeanor; they can fine you for it. Now you don't want to get fined, do you?" Lunkface was looking at him with that stupid bull look, getting ready to snort; the trick was to see how far they could jive him without him coming down on them. Hinton and Dewey turned away, as if they had lost interest in the game. Lunkface sat down. The train passed men working in the tunnel. Lunkface turned to look. Hinton leaned over and put the piece of paper and candy on Lunkface's lap so softly that he didn't even feel it. Lunkface turned around but didn't notice what they had done. The Junior had to hold his comic book close to his face to keep from showing his laugh.

When the train came to the next stop, the candy slipped and fell off and Lunkface saw what they had done to him. They all laughed, except Hector, who stilled it under the impartial leader-mask. Lunkface saw he was made a fool. He got up and made the stupid, furious face at all of them trying to decide who did it to him. They tried to give Lunkface the old I'm-innocent-officer look, but Bimbo couldn't keep it cool, cracked and giggled. Lunkface came up in front of Bimbo and reached behind his own ear, pulled his war cigarette out and held it horizontally with both hands, three inches in front of Bimbo's eyes, broke it and flung the pieces in front of Bimbo's feet and stomped on them. He turned and walked away, down to the other end of the car, facing the window, his back to the Family, having as good as told his immediate superior, *his Uncle,* and so the rest of them, to fuck themselves. Bimbo didn't know what to do; he shrugged his shoulders. In ordinary circumstances this called for group punishment, and the whole Family would come down on the offender. Bimbo sat there, puzzled, looking at Hector, waiting for his Papa's decision.

Hector saw that it had become serious and he had to do something about it. He got up. The others watched him walk down to Lunkface and put his arm around Lunkface's shoulder. They watched him trying to talk to Lunkface. Lunkface jerked away.

111

Hector patted Lunkface's shoulders. Hector offered some candy to Lunkface. Lunkface turned partly away and folded his arms on his stuck-out chest. Hector got in front of him, held Lunkface's arm, and talked. Hector kept conning Lunkface, facing back toward the Family, but talking into Lunkface's ear. The men saw that he was grinning behind Lunkface, but every time Lunkface turned to look at him, staring suspiciously out of those piggy little eyes, Hector's face became grave.

Then, suddenly, Lunkface nodded his head and turned and started coming back down the aisle toward them. Hector came with him, half-holding him back, soothing him, patting him on the back like he was calming down an animal, placating this wild man. They were all a little nervous because they knew the way Lunkface could get. The other people in the train were grinning at the whole play. Lunkface stopped in front of one, put his hands on his hips, as if to say, *What's funny?* The joker stopped grinning. After all, was this Family a show for the Other? The train came to a station and Lunkface stopped while more people got off and on; the car was filling up. When the train started, Lunkface came back to the Family. Hector followed.

Lunkface stopped in front of Hinton. That meant that Hector had selected Hinton for punishment. Hinton knew it was because of what he had said about the insignia. As soon as they stood there in front of him, Hinton put a serious face on because it wasn't a joking matter any more and the moment of trouble had come. But if Lunkface was going to lay one hand on him, he was prepared to go Something Else. Everyone respected the wild man because he didn't care for anything and there was nothing he couldn't do. Hinton had learned that a long time ago. Lunkface reached into Hinton's hatband and pulled out his war cigarette. As he did this Hinton, responding, reached into his jacket pocket, took out his pack of matches, tore one off, and held it poised to light the cigarette. Lunkface put Hinton's war cigarette into his mouth and Hinton lit it for him instantly. Lunkface puffed once, twice, blowing smoke contemptuously upward where it was shredded by the fans. Then he pinched the coal out to the floor, and stepped on it carefully, twisting the sole of his foot once, twice.

Hinton's good-looking face was wet, his lip sweat-beaded, but he would give Lunkface the satisfaction of no other expression, even though the insult of this older brother had been a strong one. But Lunkface had the right as an older brother because he was the third, after Hector and Bimbo. Hinton hoped he showed the proper expression. No one smiled or looked at him funny, though they were entitled. Lunkface stuck the war cigarette back into Hinton's band, the smudge end down, deliberately dirtying the crown of Hinton's hat.

Hector gave Lunkface another war cigarette and Lunkface brought it to Bimbo. Bimbo didn't bother to punish Lunkface, but stuck the cigarette back behind Lunkface's ear. Lunkface turned back to Hinton, and they saw that he hadn't been satisfied.

But Hector was ready for Lunkface; he proposed a game to see who was the most Man of the group. They would play chicken, and the way they would play it would be for them to stick their heads out of the window and the one that came the closest to the passing wall outside would be the winner and the Man With The Most Heart. That got them, especially Lunkface, because he had a new way to prove to them he was the biggest man, not only with the most heart, but with the biggest *cojones*. He forgot about Hinton as they turned to the window. They all participated, except Hector who was the judge, and The Junior who was back in his comic book now.

The contest was won by Hinton. He had to win it, and his fuzzy hair was scraped off the top and there was a gray smudge where the hairs were scraped, broken and whitened by the tunnel walls outside. And they admitted that this showed a great deal of heart because Hinton's kinky hair lay closest to the scalp.

The Junior had followed the adventure story through the pictures. They had fought every inch of the way; the heroes were on the way home. The heroes were, The Junior could see, the hardest men in a hard world, admirable but, he thought, he wouldn't like to be in their place, even though he envied their adventures. He sighed, turned back to the beginning as the train went through the echo-y tunnel, and the roaring darkness was getting hotter and hotter.

July 5th, 3:00—3:10 A.M.

Their train pulled into 96th Street. The doors slid open. The train waited. Everything went wrong.

The 96th Street station is an exchange point. Two lines merge there: the Broadway 242nd Street local, and the Seventh Avenue express. There are two platforms which the local and express flank. If it pulls in first, the local waits for the express. Since it had come first, their express was waiting for the local. Local and express rarely ever arrive at the same time. There is an underpass connecting the north ends of the station. On the south end of the platforms, you merely walk upstairs and are outside. On the rear end, however, you have to go downstairs first, walk through the underpass, up the staircase to the opposite side. Because it is a four-line junction, the station is always

115

full of people; because there are many people, there are some-times fights. Transit patrolmen are around all the time.

It got hotter now, the heat of the train motors drifted up. The Family was fagged out, but too tired, too uncomfortable to sleep on the sticky vinyl and foam-rubber seats. They sat, restlessly waiting for the train to move, too beat to complain. A bright, four-color, three-dimensional platform advertisement advised them that this squarish symbol was the sign of the Chase-Manhattan Bank, your symbol of confidence and friendship, and that it was 3:00 A.M. How nice would be to have already made the Times Square change-over to the Coney Island line, to be over with *that* long ride, to be back home—even if it was The Prison—sleeping. Dewey was itchy from mosquito bites; The Junior scratched at dried sweat. Now it was only a matter of drudging it through.

Hector half-dozed, facing his Family, back to the platform. Their eyes were almost shut, except for The Junior reading his comic book. A patrolling transit cop walked by the open door and glanced at the six of them sprawling. They hardly noticed him, but The Junior saw the flicker of enemy blue and made a mistake, giving Hinton the warning nudge. Hinton passed the nudge on automatically. The cop saw the motion pass along the line; there was a little hesitation in his stride. He kept going, then stopped and looked at them through one of the windows. Bimbo passed Hector the eye-sign; Hector turned and tried to see the Blue Man through the dirty window. Lunkface's shoulders hunched. Dewey folded his hands in his lap like being good in school. Bimbo's fingers plucked the tight pants-cloth free from the sweaty inner parts of his legs.

The cop passed out of sight, but his face appeared around the door at the far end of the train, giving them a quick size-up look. How much did he know? Were they looking for the men who had taken part in the meet on the plain? Did they know

116

about . . . Had they found the body? Had the girl told? Well, if she did, she was going to be just as sorry because they were all in it together. Even so, how would they know who to look for? The pins! Were they hunting the Family? Who knew? The thing to do was to sweat it out till it broke or cooled again. Let the headbusters come to them and interrogate. —Who are you? Well, the Family thought, getting the story set . . .

—No one, no one at all. Just six boys out for a ride on a hot night, sir.

—Well, where have you been?

—Here and there, up and downtown. Around. No harm in that, Officer, is there?

—None at all, sonny—the officer would say, giving the Family the thick-faced, jolly-fake, head-patting-for-the-kiddies, friendly-movie-cop-on-the-corner bit.

—Just tell me . . . you can trust me . . . where?

—Uptown and down; all around.

—Where are you from? Are you a gang?

—Not a gang; a social club, Officer.

—What school do you go to? What's your turf?

—Turf? Turf? What's that, Officer?

—Where do you live? Let me see your J.D.—I mean identification cards. And you (to Lunkface), you look old enough to be in the army. Where's your draft card?

—But I'm still a child.

—Why are you so far from home?

—But Officer, we're only out to see the world, take a little ride. After all, Wallie, our worker from the Youth Board is always after us to get out of the neighborhood, the environment. Go out, broaden your horizons, he say, get around.

—Oh? You have a Youth Board Worker? And you're *not* a gang? Let's see now, were you by some chance tied up in that big rumble uptown a few hours ago?

117

If that rumble was a few hours ago and the fuzz were still looking, it was serious. But they couldn't know about the dead bastard yet, could they? It was too soon to know, too far away from here.

—We're only sightseeing, Officer, we're not doing anything.

—Sightseeing at three in the morning? Sightseeing in a subway? Now really, boys, help me believe it.

—Well, there was this wrong-way train . . .

They began to tense.

—And now wouldn't it be better—the cop would say—to do it my way? I mean I don't want to hurt your feelings, young men, but still, and you can understand my suspicions, what with the terrible things you hear about juvenile delinquency these days.

—Oh, we understand; perfectly normal, Officer . . .

They were alert now.

—Yes, wouldn't it be better, the fuzz would say—Gentlemen, for you to go into the hood-posture; lean against that bench out on the platform there, hands on the back, feet far back and spread wide apart so you can't attack me, and that way I can frisk you and . . .

The knife! Who has the knife! Who has that fucken knife? The thought hit and their frantic looks flickered around.

Hector wink-signed. Bimbo got up and sauntered over to the door and looked out onto the platform. A few people were standing around; a woman with shopping bags had put them down and was plucking her dress free of her breasts with one hand and fanning herself with a sogged copy of a two days old *Daily News*. Bimbo leaned himself against the door, half in, half out, letting it out into his back, idle-like, so he could see inside and out. He looked down the platform at the cop's back. The buster was about two cars down now, patrolling, shoving his head into the train, trying to look unsuspicious, not making a move to alert anyone. But something made him turn around. Bimbo ducked back in, but not before he had been seen. He went back to the middle of the car and tried to see down the train's length, see through the windows, between the cars, if the buster was still looking at them. He saw nothing. He went back and popped his head back out the doorway. The cop was standing still, hands on hips, club dangling from his wrist, staring right back into Bimbo's eyes. And Bimbo tried to turn his look into a sightsee, turning his head very casually, as though there was much of interest along the platform. Bimbo's eyes saw nothing at all, not the people, not even the other side of the platform; all his attention was focused on that transit flat, who watched him, not fooled by the act. Something was wrong now. Hinton got up and drifted down to the front of the car, took his post to look through and into the cars ahead. Dewey went to the rear of the car, looking back. Lunkface was in the center, watching the other side of the tracks to the uptown platform in case the cops were coming up that way. A train was pulling into the local side there. Hector and The Junior sat.

Hector got a penny ready, stood up and drifted out, got himself a stick of gum, quick, from the machine, and drifted back in. He knew he was being watched and he began to wonder if it wouldn't have been a good idea to have removed the insignia after all. It was too easy to spot them. But the idea disturbed him and he rejected it. Still, he kept being bothered by the idea that he was being foolish. The train pulled in on the local side of their platform; people began to come across from the local to the express. Hector took off his hat and stuck out his head. The cop, four cars away, was still standing there, observing, definitely suspicious now, impatiently shifting his head to see around the people passing in front of him. Hector got back in. The doors began to close. Hector signaled. Lunkface came up and held the door open. Hinton, at the front, saw the cop come onto the train and gave the signal. They all ran out, ducking under Lunkface's arms. The door shut behind them. They were all laughing because they had outwitted that potato-head T-cop.

But that fuzz must have given out the alarm somehow, because even though one had been out-smarted into the departing train, another cop was coming, trotting in their direction, looking like a little fat blue clown that anyone of the men could have taken, but who was dangerous because he was The Law. They took evasive action: they turned and ran toward the rear. The cop, seeing the move, followed fast.

Hinton, being the fastest, ran first. He was going too fast to take the underpass exit, kept running, jumped off the end of the platform onto the tracks, and continued into the tunnel, sprinting uptown on the downtown track.

Dewey and The Junior ran toward the north end, ran down the underpass stairs, three, four, five at a time, turned the corner to the right, almost banging into the corridor wall, and were gone.

Hector, Lunkface, and Bimbo ran the same way, but at the end, following Hector's lead, they leaped onto the tracks, crossed to the right behind the iron pillars, taking care not to step on any of the rails, swung up onto the uptown platform, and ran south to the downtown end of the platform and upstairs and out into the street.

July 5th, 3:10—3:35 A.M.

Hinton ran north into the darkness; he ran as fast as he could on the railroad ties, barely seeing where he was going, getting away from the station, the platform lights, the police. The heel of his right shoe was wrenched off when it caught on a tie. He kept running. He could barely see the way ahead; his heartbeat pounded stronger; his wind was soon gone; he gasped and his right side hurt. The pulse throbbed in his eyes, wavering reality, fracturing the tunnel lights into shaky intervals. He sped past a green light and a blue one, and kept fleeing for about another hundred yards before he had to stop. He turned and looked back. He was alone. The men hadn't followed him. He could see the lights of the 96th Street station; they were much further back than he thought he had run. What had happened to the others;

121

where were they? He waited, gasping, trying to catch his breath. If they were following, they should have caught up. No one was there. What should he do? Should he go back? But that would be dancing into the arms of the headbusters who would be all over the station by now. He knew those cops—always all over everything when it was too late. Should he wait here for a while and then go back? Or keep on going to the next station? The darkness frightened him; a train might come along and roll over him. Where was the third rail? But the cops frightened him more. He could stop—just stand still—sleep. Never move again. He couldn't. He started to walk along, limping hobble-bound because of the shoe and the queer distance between the ties.

He kept stopping and listening for trains. A hole in his right sock kept widening and his toe began to rub on the leather. He listened. He heard his choky breathing distorted by the tunnel echo. Everything rumbled steadily, but seemed too faint to mean that a train was approaching. What was it then? Something dripped; something else rustled. Rats? But he was used to those. Always rats wherever he lived. He slowed. There were coffin-shaped niches painted white, along the sides. A man could stand there if trains came along. He was still sweating from his run, but at least it was cool here and it didn't bother a man to move. After a while the chilliness of the air became something felt on his skin, crawly, and that made him sure something was happening—he didn't know—as if he was in a haunted place. Foolishness. Junior kid-stuff. He laughed. The echo of that snort-laugh shocked him; distorted, he didn't know what it was for a second.

He walked on. He turned around. He could still see the station back there. How far was it to the next station? He couldn't remember how long it had taken that train to come down. Couldn't be too long, he decided. But the tunnel seemed to darken as he went; the chill increased; the steady rumble grew not so much louder, not so much as if something was coming his way, but as if the whole earth was vibrating, making weird noises.

Suppose the cops had seen him run up the tunnel? What if they had sent the word ahead to lay in wait for him? Wouldn't it be silly to keep on? All that walk to fall into their hands at the end of it. How they would laugh at him. How cool was that, how smart? Stop? Wait: sleep a little? Still, Hinton thought, you couldn't be sure. He wondered what had happened to the others. They might have gotten away and just not seen him. Maybe they thought the cops had him. The thought buckled his knees, made him tired enough to lay down. He touched the pin and the cigarette in his hat and thought, No, Papa Hector would never allow that. If they were free, they would be waiting somewhere for him. Where? Surely not at the 96th Street station. At 42nd Street where they were supposed to change for the Coney Island train. He kept going.

But if they were all captured, then it was serious. He was really alone. They would take the Family to the Station and hit them around a little, and get names and addresses, find out about the whole operation, that he had gotten away, maybe even about the man they had killed. When he got home, they would be waiting for him, like they had more than once waited for his half brother, Alonso. It might be simpler to just go back and give himself up. It might be in his favor, but it wouldn't be manly if he did. They would laugh him down and point him out as a betrayer, and he would be out of the gang, alone. And if he was alone, they would always be coming down on him. It had cost him enough trouble to get into the gang and become a brother-son. He couldn't give that up. He kept walking.

Something hit his hat. Bats! There were always bats in caves and tunnels, everybody knew that. Vampire bats! Bloodsuckers. He looked up. He shrieked—clusters of them! The shriek echoed up and down, dying slowly like the high twitters of millions of

123

bats. He cowered, kneeling on a tie, unable to move. But they didn't fly down on him. He waited. He suddenly scuttled. They didn't pounce on his back. He stopped, out of breath again, and looked up, his hand held in front of his face. He saw thick hanging paint peels, crumbling plaster, stalactites. He took off his hat. There was a big water splotch on it where some limey water had fallen. Maybe the tunnel could cave in. He shook his head to shake out the fears and walked on fast, lurching and tripping. A matter of going on, keeping calm. He would soon be to that station. He would take the train and go on down to the transfer point and meet his family there. He brushed his hat. The pin was a little off center and he tried to adjust it. He moved on, taking deep breaths to keep control. His ankle and toe hurt because of the shoe.

After a while he saw that the tracks gleamed away in a curve till they were chopped off by the swell of the turning wall. The tunnel would be in a worse darkness than here; worse because the station lights would be cut off. What if a train was bearing down on him right now and he couldn't hear it because of the tunnel wall? Did he dare go on? He half-turned. The lights of the 96th Street station were far away, barely visible now, clustered, gay, festive, tight little light strings vibrating like sparklers. He had come so far now that even the side lights illuminating the tunnel ran together at the far end. Then surely, Hinton thought, the station must be just a little further, probably just around the curve. But he stood there for a while, afraid, fighting it out, not wanting to go; afraid to leave the station lights once and for all. He was being silly. A punk kid, he told himself. It was only a matter of keeping on till he came to the station. There *couldn't* be a train coming; he'd hear it. He moved again.

The curve was longer than it appeared; it unrolled slowly as he came along it. He kept turning around to look at the 96th Street station. He tripped, fell on his palms, got up and kept going. After a while the lights were all gone. He felt alone in a darkness greater than any he had ever known before. It closed in more and more as he kept going.

There was a little light ahead. Slowly he came up on it, trying to keep close to the center pillars. He came to and passed a glass-windowed room off to the right, on the side of the uptown tracks. Men in overalls were sitting around a table, playing cards. Two were laughing. There were some beer cans on the table. It looked cool and pleasant there. He stumbled and made a noise as he passed and froze behind a pillar. They didn't seem to hear anything, since they didn't turn to look. He almost wished they'd notice him, take him in, give him a glass of beer. Not really, he thought, they were all white men, the Other. Even though it *looked* nice there, how could you be sure? He forced himself to keep walking and left the light behind.

The rails hummed. The dripping became louder, more frequent now, building up into the sound of water running. The chill became harder, a little stiffer in his face. Was there a train coming? The loneliness increased; he had never been as alone as this, never as cut off. Little sounds accumulated till there was a constant murmur keeping pace with him. He had to tell himself that his fear was a silly fear, not a man's fear. Not fear of what there was, but a little boy's fear, a terror of what wasn't. A Junior fear. He had to be a hard man, like the others—Arnold, Hector, Bimbo, Lunkface, Dewey, Ismael. These were never afraid. After all, he remembered with pride, he hadn't been spooked by that corpse and ghost jazz in the cemetery like that Junior, had he? No, he hadn't!

But by now he should have come to the station. How far could it be? And he tried to quick-march. Footsteps multiplied off the walls. Many people, or a many-footed something seemed to be walking just behind him. He stopped a second-fraction after. It was still, except for the perpetual humming. He felt as

125

though a great multitude had stopped with him too. He listened for breathing; he heard only his own. He moved on: they walked with him. He reminded himself again; it was a matter of keeping order and staying disciplined and thinking of the thing after— connecting with the men, for instance. And, anyway, he joked with himself, he was probably in the coolest part of the city. He made himself laugh but stopped. If he laughed someone might hear him. He smiled. He tried to cheer himself with the thought about the way the Family eyes would bug when he told them, "Man, let me tell you where I was and what I did."

A roaring came, filling the tunnel; he looked around for it: a train was passing on the uptown track. It was on him and the pounding and shaking and echoing was painful around him, and he jumped into one of the niches. It was childish, he scolded himself. The train was on the other side and if it had been here, he would have been killed before he had time to be scared. He stepped out between the rails and looked at the lights rattling by on the other side of the pillars. People were sitting in there; he could see the backs of their heads, and he began to run after the train, shouting at it. But no one turned around to look at him. Then the train was gone.

He stopped running. He walked on again. No, there *was* something there, someone. He thought of singing, but all he could think about were the moaning rhythms of a rock'n'roll hymn, and that was childish. Besides, if the cops *were* waiting up along the line, why give himself away? Anyway, who believed that religion shit? His mother said gospelly things all the time, but that was when she wanted something out of someone.

He had another thought. What if he had *not* gone up the same way they had come down on the train? What if he had gone up some spur that went on forever, or branched off into many tunnels? He would be lost forever, alone in this blackness. Except, of course, for the rats. They were here. He could hear them

126

rustling. And except for that . . . whatever *it* was, moving, always moving when he moved, stopping when he stopped.

He passed a blue light. Everything looked blue. What did blue lights mean? He knew what the red and green and yellow lights meant. It made his hand-skin look strange, old, covered with blue sweat. He wondered how it would be if people had blue skin. Like being dead, he thought, like not really being people. So maybe he was dead and had turned blue. The tunnel kept curving—maybe he had come back on his track and was walking in circles. Was that possible? He darted a few steps. It winded him, too quickly. Was there some kind of gas here; some kind of secret, unnoticeable poison gas? It smelled funny. The noises were louder. Or maybe the rats had an army down here. *Here* was *their* turf. Maybe they fought in gangs too? Maybe they were massing to come down on him and swarm over him. There was nowhere to hide.

He heard the sound of sobbing. The crying voices multiplied from everywhere till this whole world was filled with a chorus of sobs. Who was crying here? He stood still. And he cried now, and screamed, and waited for IT to take him. And if he shrieked, it would finally be over, because IT would know just where he was and come to get him quickly. He began to run and slipped and fell and got up and kept trotting the way he had been going. But the sound of sobbing and crying followed him with all the footsteps, mocking, filling the tunnel with weeping and crazy laughing at the same time, and the sound he couldn't help making betrayed him to the world as a coward and a weakling. What would Papa Arnold have done? What would Hector have done? He was a man, he told himself. A man! Hadn't he rumbled and held his own? Hadn't he been drunk? Hadn't he stayed cool? Hadn't he stolen and not been caught? Didn't he ball that bitch . . . too? Hadn't he wasted his man? Was that the kind of man that little-babied so easy? Didn't he learn long ago that to

127

tear-up is to get laughed at, even by your own mother, or that motherfucker, Norbert, his mother's boy friend. It was better in this world to dry your tears before they left your eyes, and stifle the howl-sounds from the earliest on, because it was only going to get you put down.

But IT didn't come as easy, or get anything over with. There was no one here—nothing at all. Only the blackness, and he was part of it, and he was more alone than he had ever been. And now he became like a little baby, making howl sounds that he had never permitted himself to make. He heard himself and promised that as soon as he caught his breath, he was just going to start laughing at himself for the kind of Dominator he hadn't been. Just suppose that the others had gotten away too, and were behind him, jiving him, sneaking up on him, to watch him, to test him, the way they had tested him when he had first come into the gang. That stopped him. He turned and looked back. He called out, "All right, I know you're there. Come on out. I was only joking."

He caught his breath and listened. He heard nothing but rustling and rumbling and humming. He saw nothing but a few big water bugs scuttle in and out of the circles of light.

He was muttering, "Fuck them, fuck it, fuck them." And he got madder and madder and he was yelling with rage at what that mothering Family was doing to him, and he tore off his hat and threw it down and stamped on it, and the pin, and he went over to the wall and finger-wrote in the crusted dirt, "Hinton D. shits on the MF Dominators from the Father and the Mother on down, and on all his brothers."

And he thought, all right, he would just pack himself into a niche and wait. He didn't know what he'd wait for, but he would wait. He would curl up and put his head on his knees and wait till the cops, or his Family, or IT came and got him. He would do just that because he hadn't been in a quiet spot for days and days now.

But what he had just done terrified him, because it so completely cut him off, and though they couldn't see it, it was as though the Family would somehow *know* what he had done, and he would be out, but good. He got his hat, straightened it, fidgeted with the pin, taking it off, brushing it, pinning it back on the hat, straightening the damaged war cigarette. He wiped off what he had written with his sleeve and took out the Magic Marker and wrote, instead, the Name of his Family, to show that there was no place in this city, even this tunnel, where his Family was not or had not been. The act comforted him and he went on.

And after a while, he came around another curve and there was the station. He slowed and sneaked up on it, looking to see that there were no cops on the platform and that no one spotted him. He looked around and when the few people that were there didn't notice, he climbed the ladder at the platform's end and was on the 110th Street station.

Now it was only a matter of getting to the Times Square stop and changing for the Coney Island train. He would meet the Family there. If they had gotten away, that's where they would meet him. He was sure.

He jittered. He was ashamed of himself. He had gone through something he didn't understand. He was glad no one had seen him, but he felt as if it was there, marked on his face, on his clothes for everyone to know what he was. He asked himself, how many of the others could do what he had done—walk through that darkness alone? The answer didn't comfort him.

After a while the downtown train came and he got on. In the clear train light, mirrored in a window he saw that his clothes were water stained, plaster smeared, spotted all over with chalk. He didn't sit yet. The back of his right sock was rubbed away and the flesh of his ankle was abraded raw. The shoe was still held together by the narrow band of frayed leather and he had to keep his toe cramped when he walked. One of his palms was scraped bloody and they were both dirty. He took off his hat. Water had mottled it. The shine of his insignia was dulled, and his cigarette was partly split and tobacco sprayed out over the band. He remembered what Lunkface had done to him. He wondered if Lunkface was enough of a man to walk through that darkness. Of course: Lunkface would come through, but strong. The best thing in life was to be like Lunkface.

Hinton sat down. He leaned back, unhappy, uncomfortable, not daring to sleep in case he missed his stop.

July 5th, 3:10—3:35 A.M.

Dewey and The Junior escaped the transit cop by bounding down the stairs. They swung off right into a short underpass smelling of piss. They pounded a few steps and cut off to the right again, bouncing up the staircase to the platform. They heard Hector, Bimbo, Lunkface chasing behind them. Across the tracks, on the downtown side, the train had pulled out; they could see the transit-chaser wheezing after them in a slow, clumsy pursuit, and it was a miracle they weren't seen.

A train was waiting on the uptown local tracks. They whipped in and sat down away from the doors, backs to the window, half-scrunched down to avoid being seen, not looking behind them. The Junior pulled out his comic book and stared at it, trying to look like he'd been reading it for hours. He didn't see a thing;

131

he couldn't read past one panel which showed a three-colored Greek warrior with his raised spear, ready to shove it into a skin-wearing enemy's throat. He kept expecting to see, out of the edges of his eyes, the great black flat feet of the headbusters coming to close in on him. Dewey pursed his lips like whistling, but didn't make a sound; he sat there, blowing air. He tried to keep his hands classroom-folded, but they fidgeted, picking at him, finding dirty places to brush off and creases to straighten out, refolding and beginning again. Where were the others; probably in one of the other train cars.

The doors closed. The train started. They didn't know where they were going, they didn't even dare to look up at the destination sign. The thing was to do nothing for a little while; surely Hector would show. The train came to the next station, 103rd Street. The Junior wondered if they had come downtown this way. They hit 110th Street. The Junior became confused. The next stop was 116th and The Junior knew they were going a different way. But the third stop was 125th Street. They knew they had passed this station on the way down, but this was out in the open, high up on a trestle. They were confused now. They got up and went from car to car, looking for the others and found that now they were alone. Had the fuzz captured the others? They sat down and tried to figure out what they should do.

Dewey thought it would be a good idea to ride on for a while and then to go back. After all, he told The Junior, they knew—to change for the Coney Island train at Times Square—the BMT it was, Dewey remembered. They would go on for a while, cross over and double downtown, and meet the others where you get the Coney Island train. They would wait there for a while; if the others didn't show, that could only mean that the busters had really taken them and they would make it home themselves.

They sat for a while. Now they were safe and The Junior

132

could concentrate. He turned a page, forgot what he had been reading, and looked back to the point where the Greek warrior, muscled and big chested, was putting the spear point to the enemy's gut. The Junior saw himself putting the spear point to the enemy fuzz—a bull in blue armor wearing a steel helmet, with a New York City seal shield, coming down the platform, charging down on them. The Greek heroes were climbing mountains and the enemy was japping for them along a ridge. They had piles of rocks in ready-to-cut nets, logs to roll down, which could be set on fire. The leader of the Greeks, cool in a gold glinting helmet with a wavy-fur crest, was trying to parley with the savage leader of the hill tribesmen, only they wouldn't negotiate. The hero said, well, they had come in peace and they wanted to pass in peace, and they were marching through, and if we have to waste you, we waste. If you come down on us, it's on your head because we wanted peace. Remember.

The Junior looked up and saw that the station was 137th Street. He poked Dewey and wanted to know if they shouldn't change yet. Dewey was no help; he was the older brother and he should have given counsel, but instead he said for The Junior to read his literature while he tried to figure it out. The Junior tried to interest Dewey in the book, but Dewey snorted and his eyes were scornful behind his thick, horn-rimmed glasses. "Spears, Man? Who uses spears? I mean the Powerman, or the Atomman, he blows a man's arms off with them cosmic rays; things like that. Or the Rocketman. They punch a bleedy hole in you, big as a melon. Spears? Man!" and he turned away.

The Junior asked if maybe they shouldn't take out their war cigarettes and take off their pins. Dewey looked indecisive and didn't say anything. They couldn't decide it, but they knew that their situation might be desperate. What if they had been spotted? Finally, Dewey said if they did that and nothing happened . . . Remember the way Hinton had been put down.

133

Those pins, they were the Family sign and they stood or fell with their signs, and it was the mark that a man belonged—they were one. To take them off was to be like any heartless slob coolie who wouldn't take chances; without important affiliations. And so they must go along with the whole bit. It made them men. The Junior nodded and agreed. It was like those Greeks and their crazy haircrest helmets. Wouldn't it be wonderful if the Family wore helmets like that? The Junior agreed, and said he was only talking, for the sake of argument, and that he was patriotic.

The Junior was fourteen, Dewey reasoned, and that meant he wouldn't have much trouble anyway if he got caught; he knew that. True, Dewey was sixteen, but then, what could they really prove? What could they *really* prove? None of them had the slice on them. "What do they know?" Dewey asked. "I mean, man, really, like what do they *know?*"

"Nothing," The Junior said. "I was only talking for the sake of the argument." They felt a little better for having decided to keep on wearing the insignia. It showed that they were men, and more, men in danger, and they were upholding their rep and that rep consisted, among other things, of having killed their man.

"Look at this," The Junior showed Dewey.

"Man, that's punk-stuff," Dewey said, but having nothing better to do, he looked at the comic book with The Junior. They followed the story. The heroes marched through deserts; they marched over mountains; they marched in the rains and in snows. They fought every inch of the way. The artist was good because the silver of the spears almost glinted and the red of the blood stood out very clearly.

134

July 5th, 3:10–3:35 A.M.

Hector and Lunkface vaulted over the turnstiles, one hand on the turn bars. Bimbo scuttled after, going down and under the stile bars. They climbed the stairs, two and three at a time, and were out at 93rd Street and Broadway. Because it was the easiest way to go, they turned right and ran downhill in the direction of the Hudson River, though they didn't know where they were or where they were going. They passed chalked-up signs announcing whose turf this was, but they didn't stop to read. Bimbo looked behind to see if that cop had followed. They were in the clear. They didn't run; to run was to bring down Law. When they had crossed the street, Lunkface took off his handkerchief, threw the war cigarette away, folded the handkerchief

135

around the insignia and put it into his pocket. Hector wanted to know what he thought he was doing.

"Man, I'm taking it off, that's what I'm doing. I'm not going to be spotted," Lunkface told Hector.

"You can't do that."

"You think I'm going around and making a show of myself so I'll get picked up? You think I'm going around and saying, here, Fuzzy John, here is Lunkface, sir. Come and get me and run me in, sir. You think I'm going to wear the sign so that the armies who hold this territory can worry us? No, man, oh no." His face was angry; Lunkface was working himself up into a temper.

"Cool it, man; cool it, sonny," Hector told Lunkface.

"I'm cool, man. Who says I'm not cool? I am like ice."

"I thought we swore. We're a family, a war party. We move as an army."

"But man, it does not pay to advertise. It's cost us, man."

"Who gives the orders here? Doesn't Father know best?"

The invocation didn't work on Lunkface. "Hector . . ."

"Call me Father, you hear?"

"I'm not challenging you, man, but look. We won't go for ten minutes without the fuzz buzzing us and tailing us. I mean they *know,* man. They know all about tonight and their eyes are out in all directions. I've been busted before. You think I'm happy with it, Father? I'm tired of being shoved here and there and I got to make it back to that homeland."

Hector saw that the more he talked, the wilder Lunkface got. It was pointless to reason and say that their getting chased had nothing to do with the pins, or the rumble, or the stomping. And after all, you couldn't tell; maybe the word *really was* out. Bimbo watched one face and then the other to see who had won it, so Hector knew that he had to make it look as if he had given the order, or he would lose his position. They crossed a street and were by a park. They were on a little rise; ahead, park be-

136

yond, cars were going up and down on the West Side Highway.

"You might be right, but this is not the way to do it," he told Lunkface. "There are ways of having your say . . ."

"We don't have conference time . . ."

"We'll talk about it later, you understand me, son?" and Hector lingered on *son*.

"I understand you, Father," and Lunkface drew out the word father. "I understand you the most. I mean you're a man, and I'm a man. I know you and you know me. All right. We'll mediate it later."

Hector turned and valuted over a low, iron fence that ran alongside the grass. He walked a few steps and turned around.

"All right, children, we take off the signs," he told them.

Bimbo followed Hector, but Lunkface didn't; he just waited. Bimbo looked back at Lunkface. Lunkface shrugged and turned away. Bimbo kneeled in front of Hector; he felt silly because he was the only one. Hector took the cigarette out of Bimbo's hatband and put it into the red cigarette case; he took out his own cigarette and put it away. "Unpin," he told Bimbo. Bimbo looked a little uncomfortable, but shrugged his shoulders. Hector unpinned Bimbo and took off his own hat and removed the Mercedes-Benz three-point star pin. He put them into his pocket. They came back to where Lunkface, trying to look detached and contemptuous, was waiting. Lunkface was a little sorry for what he had brought about. He hadn't thought he would feel it this much. Of course this wouldn't have happened if *he* was the Father. But on the other hand he didn't have the kind of smartness, the special power. He couldn't be clever like Hector or Arnold. Nor was this the time or the place to take the Fathership over. If he had taken control it would have meant a fight, and a fight would bring the fuzz.

They all turned into the park and went south, mostly because Hector went that way. They had lost the identity of oneness and

137

were almost like three squares, coolies, three men who no longer had the special power. They all felt uncomfortable, detached, somehow—naked, like any three who happened to know one another and be dressed alike. They didn't talk. Beyond the highway they could see the Hudson River, a broad, shimmering path of floating lights, and the darker Palisades looming over the water, and the escarpment light-spangled. To their left, the apartment buildings lining the Drive towered over them. A few last tired firecrackers were going off; abortive rockets sputtered defectively.

Hector said that they would continue to walk south, cut back in the direction they had come, take the train further down the line, continue and meet the others, if they hadn't been picked up, at Times Square. They kept walking. Every thirty feet or so there was a bench under a lamp, but no one was sitting on any of them. Names were carved all over the bench woodworks: gang titles, names of gang members, instructions to one another. The park seemed deserted.

She was sitting about a half a block ahead of them. Her bench was screened from the river by bushes, but she could still see the sky. She was a little drunk and half-sleepy; she kept lolling on the bench and dozing and waking. She had seen great sheaves of fire exploding in the sky, fire-fruits blooming, stalks of flame efflorescing, blazing leaves had grown in the sky. She didn't quite know if something was really there or, because she was wearing her silver-rimmed reading bifocals, the flowering lights were out of her imagination, distorted and wild when seen through these lenses. But altogether, it had been a lovely Fourth. From time to time she reminded herself that it was late, very late, and she should be going home now or they would be worrying about her.

And she remembered, again, it was the Fourth, the Glorious Fourth, the safe and sane Fourth, the drunken Fourth. Not that

138

she was drunk, because she had only taken a few at the hospital where she was a nurse; she hardly ever touched the stuff. And before you knew it, here she was, sitting on a bench in the Riverside Drive Park to sober—to clear her head. The wind coming in off the river was blocked by the bushes, so it was all still and smelled seafishy and seaweedy and of barge oil and ocean garbage. She thought sleepily of moving to another bench where she would get the cooling breezes, where no bushes stood in the way, where a woman could cool the heat of her face and let the winds play around her. But every time she got ready to move, it was too much trouble. Her legs wouldn't function right; her big pocketbook was much too heavy. Maybe it was her week's pay; maybe it was the small bottle of medicinal whiskey. She giggled, moved, and the bench creaked. She was a big woman.

Bimbo saw her first and nudged Hector. In the light from the park lamp, they could see that her head lolled back and her eyes were closed. Her glasses had slipped down her flat nose and she had a silly smile that distorted her big, flat cheeks. Her legs were sprawled apart, they closed and opened, shuttling, seeming to weave. Her head rolled a little and she kept smiling at some private joke. They saw she had great thick calves, but her ankles were narrow, almost bony; her skirt was hitched halfway up her white-stockinged thighs. Her nurse's cap, held on by one hairpin to her blond or white hair—they weren't sure which—hung loosely over her forehead.

Lunkface's body tensed; he became uncomfortable in his tight pants. He looked around—no one in sight at all. Bimbo, knowing Lunkface, was watching him and grinning. Show Lunkface a little and he was gone, Bimbo thought. That was because he didn't have a steady woman. Only Hector kept a serious face. He didn't like the whole thing.

Lunkface walked ahead. The others followed. They stood in front of her. She didn't seem to notice. Lunkface squatted and looked up under her skirt, stood up and shook his hand up and down, loose-wristedly. Hector shook his head. Bimbo looked from one to the other. They whispered. Hector said it would be a foolish act. Besides, what did they want with an old woman, someone old enough to be your mother?

"Like it's whiptight and singing for it in my pants, man, and I got to, now now now now," Lunkface said.

"Don't you ever get enough? Stay cool. Don't we have enough trouble? Stay cool."

"Stay cool, stay cool," Lunkface mimicked. "That's easy for you to say; you have a woman and get it all you want."

Bimbo said, "Man, this old cunt, she should be home. And if she's here, she's asking for it, coming out like this. Don't she know the parks, they're not safe after dark?"

Lunkface said, "And she's going to get it, but good."

"Now cool it," Hector snapped.

"Now, man. *Now*. You can't jive me out of this," Lunkface said. "If you want to cut out go ahead. I'm Down to Kill and I'm going to have it, but good."

She opened her eyes and dimly saw the three standing in front of her. Men. Boys. Young men. Only the one in the middle seemed to have any light on his face; that was because he was standing straighter than the others. She liked his posture. She saw, over her glasses, that he had a beautiful face and blond, wavy hair curling down from his set-back hat. "You're a pretty one," she told Hector. "A pretty boy." She shook her head and closed her eyes.

"Lady, are you all right?" Hector asked her.

"And a pretty voice you have, so soft it is," she said, opened her eyes and smiled on the middle one. This time she noticed his two friends. They were darker-skinned. The short, squat one was a muddy light brown and had a little fuzzy mustache and looked Indian-faced. The other one was bulky-big, quite dark, ugly, Negro-faced.

140

Bimbo nudged Hector again. Hector shook his head and moved as if to keep on walking, but Lunkface wouldn't move. Hector saw the way it was going to be. He knew when Lunkface got that way he was uncontrollable. You could shoot him and he wouldn't notice. Rather than risk another loss of face, Hector decided he would anticipate Lunkface and do what he wanted to do. "Well," he said; "The family that lays together stays together." Bimbo giggled. "Not here," Hector whispered to the two of them. Lunkface adjusted the hard tightness in his groin so that it sat a little better in his pants, up against his stomach.

"Lady, you need a little help?" Hector said gently, conning her.

She opened her eyes and looked at the beautiful boy in the middle. She made patting motions on the bench beside her and nodded to him and told him to sit down beside her. Hector gave her his short, full smile; he was always very smooth; he never frightened them; he never got that stupid, lustful look like Lunkface. Hector was beginning to get a little excited himself. He sat down beside her. Lunkface sat down on the other side of her. Bimbo went around to the back of the bench. She put her arm around Hector and told him, "You know, I've got two nephews, one prettier than the other, and you remind me of them." And she grabbed him close to her, pulling his head down a little. The arm flesh puffed out of her tight sleeveband and against his cheek; her body was warm; Hector was surprised at how strong she was.

Lunkface put one hand on her thigh, just above her knee, and was kneading the flesh there. She became aware of it, looked down and saw the dark hand on her white stocking and said, "Get your hand off; what kind of a woman do you think I am?" Bimbo grinned behind her. Lunkface didn't remove his hand, but just slid his grip to the inside of her leg. She turned back to Hector, but told Lunkface, without looking at him, "Get your hand off."

141

"Lady, you feeling all right? Lady, you need a little help?" Lunkface asked, trying to sound smooth like Hector.

"I'll bet that all the girls like you, a beautiful boy like you," she said to Hector, holding him around the neck. His neck began to feel abraded. "You get them girls, don't you sweetie? A sweet boy like you?"

Hector didn't like being controlled. The smell of liquor on her breath bothered him; from close-up you could see that she was even older than they thought. He leaned away. Lunkface slipped his other arm around her waist and was trying to reach around to squeeze her breast. Bimbo was leaning over her and trying to see down the front of her uniform.

She sat up suddenly and made waving motions with her hand, as if she were brushing insects away. She stood up suddenly, her hand still holding Hector, and he was pulled up with her. "Get away, Nigger," she said to Lunkface, and he sat there, stunned for a second. As she stood, they saw she was an enormous woman, about two inches bigger than Lunkface, and much wider. Bimbo laughed. Lunkface rose slowly, ready to start punching her in the face for the unjustness of the insult. He was American, a Puerto Rican of Spanish descent, but she had turned and said to Hector, still holding him, "Come on, little baby, let's go off somewhere where we can be alone and you can tell me all about your adventures with the little girlies." And she giggled and lurched a little, and steadied herself on Hector and almost knocked him down, pulled him along for a few steps on the walk, and then off onto the grass and they were walking through the bushes and onto another part of the lawn. Lunkface nodded at Hector to go ahead. Bimbo nodded, too. They followed.

Her legs wobbled a little on the grass and her shoes shone white on the dark lawn. She leaned on Hector and held him closer and closer; her body was hot; her other hand stroked his slim-muscled arm, feeling through the jacket, stroking over and over again, telling him how cute he was, as they walked toward a grassy, half-enclosed grove. Bimbo and Lunkface followed, looking around to make sure that there was no one else in the park. Their faces had set into grins, though they weren't even aware that they were grinning. They would fix her when they got her a little way off; they would show her; they would show her who was a nigger; they would show her what men were like. That old bitch. They came to an open space.

Bimbo and Lunkface separated and came at her from two angles and behind. Lunkface was determined to be the first one. Hector, who didn't really want her at all, knew they were coming up, had turned toward her and was standing still while her hands were rubbing his chest, and she started to say things like it wasn't nice to have things to do with those young girls. She knew, she was a nurse. They were all evil nowadays, and diseased and dirty-minded, and they did terrible things, and did he do those things, those dirty French things, with those diseased little sluts, and was he a man yet?

Hector told her he was a man, his face cool and set, and he said he had heart and everything else that was required. She said that of course he was a man, what a pretty man he was, but she didn't care about his heart, and she laughed and laughed, and it made Hector angrier because he was sure this old bitch was laughing at him. But she swung him tight to her and her arms were around him and half-smothering his face into her talcum-smelling breast-cut, and she was rubbing him against her and he couldn't get free to do much to her, even if he wanted to, and he began to try to jerk free to do it, because he was the *man,* and it was the *man* who did things, not the woman, not some woman they were going to give it to anyway. Great waves of heat emanated from her and her face shone and glowed and she looked younger and Hector had never felt such heat from a human being.

She took his hand in hers and was rubbing it all over her big breast and he tried to pull free, but she was strong. She kept telling him what a fine thing it was for a young man like him to have things to do with a fine, mature woman like she was. The other hand was holding him close and stroked hard all up and down his back, from the back of his head down to the bottom of his buttocks, and she squeezed him there, almost painfully, because she was such a big-handed, powerful woman that she held one buttock in one hand like he was a child. And her bag was hooked onto that wrist and was banging him in the back every time she stroked up and down. And she was beginning to thump his body against her, and swaying more and more, hitting at him, and he could feel himself hard and erect and uncomfortable in his tight pants, but he couldn't pull free so he could swing it out and show her *hombre*. But she was so frenzied for him now that she didn't let him go, and it was getting him wild with anger and frustration because he was being choked and was sweating and was covered with her sweat.

Lunkface was right behind her, on her right, and his eyes were small, mean, almost drunk, his face frozen into the lust-grin. Bimbo was on the other side of her and his expression was almost idiotic. Lunkface signaled for Hector to step free. But, Hector thought, angrier and angrier, who was Lunkface to signal *him*? Wasn't there a natural order to these things? Father down to the last son? So he pretended he liked the woman and put his lips to hers and began to move with her motion and feel of his own volition and went up and down and swayed with her. Lunkface came around and put his hand to Hector's shoulder and tried to pull him away. Bimbo was giggling. They were all moving around in the dimness, stumbling on the uneven ground. It wasn't completely dark here because there were too many lights shining all around, from the buildings on the hill, from the shore across the river, from the lamps set along the drive and in the park. She kept muttering little endearments to Hector, and try-

144

ing to do something about it and they were just not connecting right. He was repulsed by her because she was pouring out sweat and heat now and the powder stink was stronger and she smelled like a hospital because she was a nurse, to say nothing of the liquor stink on her. Bimbo was sure she must have liquor in her bag and was trying to get to it. She felt the tug and broke loose suddenly and swung at Bimbo; he just ducked under her swing, giggling at the whole thing.

But her motion sent Hector back a little. She turned back to him and said, "Sweetheart, get rid of these Niggers, will you?" and reached. Lunkface, hot and strong now, came on with the heat in him so fierce that nothing could stop him, no loyalty, no sense of precedence, of right and wrong; only the feel of it in her would make it right, and he unzipped his pants and grabbed for her. She tried to shove her way clear, but they were at her, push-ing at her, pulling at her clothes, ripping the buttons of her uni-form loose, the three of them working as one now—Bimbo to trip her, Hector to help hold her arms, and Lunkface to fuck her—holding, stroking her, trying to maneuver. And she was half-angry, half-willing now, and by this time the need for sex had mingled with the drunkenness and she became a little drunk with the want of it. And so she let herself be pushed over by the boys and fell gently, onto the soft grass, and onto her back, her legs starting to draw up and open, and she giggled a little and said, "Don't tear now, sweetie, don't tear," and her hands swung and grabbed Lunkface like no other woman had ever grabbed him before, one hand on his jacket lapel, tearing it a little, and the other powerful hand ripped downward on his pants, pulling them down with one astonishing jerk of her hand, tearing the cloth that held the clasp that fastened his pants.

Hector was sitting cross-legged beside them, his penis in his hand, ready to jump on as soon as Lunkface was through. Bimbo was stretched out, prone, his face an inch away from

Lunkface's and the nurse's faces, peering at them. His penis was out, too; he was lying arse-arched, rubbing it in the dew-cool grass. They were on the verge of connecting. And she, her great and powerful legs splayed out, was trying to adjust herself away from her undergarments so that the boy could do it, but he squirmed so much, and she laughed a little, feeling somehow, drunk or not, it might be wrong, but still, the excitement was so strong in her and she wanted it so badly, that she knew she was going to take on the three of them, and then the three of them again, and then—then, it might just be enough.

But Bimbo couldn't leave it alone. He thought maybe she had money and liquor in her bag. His head was propped up on one hand and he reached out with the other hand to slip her pocketbook toward him, pulling the strap along her arm till it was close. Then he unsnapped the bag. She heard the *click*. The sound made her angry and she jerked her hand away quickly and turned toward Bimbo, half on her side, almost spilling Lunkface off, and shouted, "Let that alone, you little thief!"

Lunkface, his moment spoiled, raised himself up on one arm and hit her in the face with the other hand to make her lie still. She turned and her knee smashed up and caught Lunkface in the side and knocked him off, onto the grass. She sat up and her hand shot out and her backhand caught Lunkface, and his head rang as he tumbled back to the grass. She was trying to get to her feet when Bimbo dived at her from his knees. She rose, Bimbo holding onto her shoulders, turned, and shrugged him off. Hector was laughing when she turned in his direction and whaled him with the flailing pocketbook, knocking him back, and at the same time, she began to deliver a long, screaming tirade about a woman not being safe anywhere, and these spics, these Niggers, these foreigners, were no respectors of age, or motherhood, of gray hairs, of gentility.

It stopped them for a second and they stood there like little children while she scolded them and they almost backed off, but the voice began to get shriller and they couldn't let themselves be put down like that, not by a woman, and Lunkface tried to hit her in the mouth to shut her up, but he half missed in the dimness and she was knocked to her knees by his body and began to scream "RAPE" in a voice that was louder than celebration explosives and was going to reach from here to the other side of the Hudson and back, and if there were fuzz within a few blocks, they had to hear this wild old bitch.

Hector scrambled away and got to his feet. Bimbo was getting up and Lunkface was trying to recover from his swing to take her out again. She swung out with her bag and caught Bimbo in the face and his nose began to run blood over his mustache, making him madder, and he was reaching into his pocket for the slice. Who was this old cunt to do this to him, a man, to bloody a good man like him?

She was standing there, her uniform open, her ripped slip bunched around her waist, one great breast free of her brassiere, and swinging in time to her lashing out, while she kept shouting "RAPE." And Hector was trying to pull Lunkface away. Lunkface hadn't pulled up his pants yet and was trying to launch himself at her. Her thick legs were planted far apart as Bimbo came up behind her to push the slice into her and prick her with something real when the wide-swinging bag caught him in the ear and knocked him down again and he lost the knife in the grass and he groped for it, getting kicked under all those legs.

"RAPE!" she boomed out, her cap bouncing on her gray head, still held on by the hairpin. "RAPE," she woke the dead. Hector charged, head down, but her open hand cracked his face and he went down. "RAPE!" she screamed, and they knew it was time to clear. Hector crawled away, scrambled to his feet, and tried to run away from her. He yelled for them to follow him. Bimbo ran around her, shaking his fist at her, and began to run with Hector.

147

But Lunkface wouldn't give it up. She came to him. He tried to grab her. She slapped him, one and two, screaming "RAPE," all the time without a stop and knocked him tripping over his pants which were still around his ankles. He tried to crawl away. "RAPE!" she bellowed and kicked him with her white shoe. "RAPE RAPE RAPE!"

"I'll kill you. I'll kill you," Lunkface screamed while she kept on beating down at him, dancing around him, kicking his bare arse, her arms flailing, her bag swinging, her tit bouncing. The others came back from either side, hit her, and that knocked the wind out of her. And she shrieked a soundless "rape." They grabbed Lunkface, pulled him to his feet, and started to run away. But she caught her breath and was screaming again. Her glasses were gone and she followed after the half-seen shapes. Bimbo and Hector were ahead of Lunkface now. They couldn't hang around and wait for the Busters to come. And Lunkface hopped, trying to run, trying to pull up his pants, wanting to get away from her. But he wasn't able to do it.

But the fuzz had heard and come up in prowl cars on two sides. Bimbo and Hector ran into a bluesuit who stiffed Bimbo in the wind with his night stick and Bimbo doubled down on his hands and knees and began to vomit. The cop's other hand shot out and knocked off Hector's hat and closed around his thick, wavy hair, bringing him up short and almost making his eyes pop out of his head, and his feet slid out and he was held up on his toes by the Fist's grip. Another cop wheeled his patrol car onto the grass behind them and came running out and caught Lunkface, belted him on the bare behind with his pistol barrel, pulled him up, and made him stand there, his hands folded on top of his head, his pants still down around his ankles.

"Pull up your pants," a cop said. Lunkface bent. Another cop kicked him. He pitched forward. A third cop pulled him up by the arm and threw him toward the others. More cars came and illuminated them in the headlights. Fuzz blanketed the place.

148

They asked her what was the matter. She was all teary. Her shaky hand held the lapels of her uniform together while she told a story of taking some air and being set on by these sex-mad hooligans. Wasn't a woman, any woman, even a mother, a grandmother, safe anywhere anymore? What wouldn't these beasts stop at? The cop smelled liquor on her breath, but seeing Lunkface standing there like that made him mad and he nodded sympathetically and patted her on the shoulder and told her, there, there, she was safe now. They would get what was coming to them.

Bimbo and Lunkface didn't say anything; they knew it was pointless. But Hector tried to explain that she had given them the old come-on, and that so infuriated one cop that he knocked Hector back and forth and bloodied his mouth and broke his nose and knocked a tooth loose. One of the cops said mildly, leave him alone, but the others were mad—boys assaulting a woman like this. And they slapped the boys around a little more as they herded them into the patrol cars. The boys said nothing else. And so they went down to the station house where it was going to be much worse.

July 5th, 3:45—4:30 A.M.

"My, what a pretty pin you have," the voice sweet-toned into Hinton's ear as he went by. It was like casting dirt on the mark of a warrior: filthy honey. He half-saw the fag out of the corner of his eye, cut him, and moved on. They always bothered you; they never let you rest. Soon he would go back to the BMT train. If the Family wasn't there by now, he would go home alone. The Family had probably been taken and he alone was left. Or he had missed them and they had gone straight home. He couldn't hang around here with these people bugging him. He moved.

He wandered through underground galleries twisting in and out through the Times Square subway complex, staring around him, puzzling out the direction signs. You could get lost so easily

150

here. Four train lines here—hidden rooms—long tile-lined corridors. He wondered if the fag who whispered into his ear, seeming to be a part of the passing crowd, was the same fag who had given him the come-on twice before that night. He wondered if he should take off the pin. But it was his mark; it showed he was not like the Other. He wore it proudly now. Still, you had to be careful because the fuzz covered everything: club-swinging patrolmen stood around in twos; plain-clothes gumshoes crept around and cased the creeps. That fag might even have been an enticer from the Law looking to fat up his arrest record. They *would* pick on a no-pay stranger.

He had come down from 110th Street without trouble, and gotten off at the right stop asking where the BMT Coney Island train was. They had told him where to make the change. He had walked over to the right platform, but none of the Family had come yet. He had stood around the almost empty platform, trying to look inconspicuous. When a few trains went by, he was sure a multi-hardhand was giving him the eye on suspicion. And still the Family didn't come. He got hungry and filled his pockets from the vending machines. He had eaten about fifteen penny chocolates and two fruit-nut bars, but it wasn't enough. He had two Cokes in paper cups from an automatic machine to help the candy down and then he had run out of coins. The newsstand on the platform was closed; he couldn't get any change; he had to sit, stand, then wander, limping because of his right foot, from one end of the platform to the other, looking around, always alert. What if the Family was here, looking for him, and he kept missing them, behind pillars, kiosks, anywhere? A rag-bag gang of boys, more a mob, went by giving him the lookover. How without style, discipline, they were, he thought—how coolie— but he looked in another direction because they were wild. Something else, every one of them, smouldering and ready to catch fire and swarm over him if they suspected contempt.

151

It got hotter and hotter and it was hard to hang around. He perspired and couldn't move right because his clothes were held by a film of sweat-slick all over his body. He could smell himself; the only air that got stirred up was made by the trains coming by. After a while the heat almost made him dance with the itch.

Then somebody laid down a barrage of big firecrackers at one end of the platform and people were running and yelling, and a lot of transit cops came charging down, and he had to take off fast because the Headbusters would stiff anyone who looked like he might have set it off. He couldn't run right because his shoe was busted and his heel was bloody and he ran in a long hop, skip, and a shortstep, and he hoped the shoe wouldn't fall off because he couldn't walk around in his socks. He ran up a flight of stairs, turned once, ran down a tile-lined passage, and then found himself in a dead end with a door at the end marked WOMEN. But, instead of being closed, it was half-open and he ran in to hide. The place was crowded; all kinds were there— men, women, kids, fags, girls, lesbos, young and old. The air was heavy with a sweet-smoke smell and he knew what that was —marijuana. Alonso used to take it before he had gone on to better things. Someone had a portable radio and it was playing that wild, high-voiced savage stuff, jazzed, big-beat tribal shout-singing with falsetto choruses, right out of the jungle. But it was oddly cooler here, maybe because of the tile walls. Everyone looked like they were something else, from another world. Hinton couldn't place it; it wasn't only the costumes. But he didn't dare to stare because they might interpret it as an offense and then . . .

A huge stud stood up against the wall. He was brutal, six foot six or so, wide, with a look on his face like the world had to dig *him*. He looked like someone out of the old past wearing an archaic black leather jacket decorated with bars, stars, leaves, and zipper-gear. He wore a visored speedboy cap, engineer stomp-boots, blond sideburns down to the lower part of his stick-out ears, unfashionable blue jeans, and he had gloves stuck into the epaulets of his jacket. Nobody dressed like that any more, Hinton thought scornfully, but the man was just too big to put down. Next to the giant was a grinning young boy wearing a black suit; it took a second to see it was a girl.

They all stopped and turned to look at Hinton, no one saying anything at all. There was a grunting noise, a slurping noise, a panting wheeze, all the sounds going on steadily like machinery. Toilets flushed and a cry of pain, or pleasure, sounded hollowly off the walls. Hinton moved on in like he had been coming here in the first place. He was scared but he kept his face set and hard because to show them fear would mean being dragged down.

"Here's one," a voice said.

Somebody answered, "Well, he'll want it white."

The giant pushed off from the tile wall and came to him, took his arm by the elbow and led him to the back. As he passed the first booth, the door was open. A girl was sitting. She was Negro, naked. She sat in the toilet seat, legs crossed, her elbow on her knee and her face, which moved up and down while she chewed gum, rested in her hand. Five or six booths were closed.

They took Hinton back to a booth in which there was a tired-looking little white girl. She was very skinny; her chest bones showed and she was almost breastless. Her blonde hair had un-dyed black raying through it. She smiled and stood up; her pubic hair was platinumed. She wore low, gold lamé sneakers. She smiled. The giant's hand opened and he said, "Three." Hinton dug in and felt three dollars out of his pocket because to show more was foolish. Even though he didn't want to, he wasn't going to get out of it unless he got it over with, and he could never show them he wasn't man enough.

A hand pushed him in. The door closed behind him; it was

half-dark here. There was a quick fumbling; they came together; it was stifling; urine had been spilled all over the place; he was gasping; his feet slid a little; he turned his head away and saw that her clothes were hanging on a hook at the side. She said a few words and panted and made a quick moan-sound; he was dizzied as their feet shuffled through muddy floor-grit. He thought he would keel over. When it was finished she moved away and sat down on the toilet seat and was pulling down toilet paper and began to wipe herself and he wasn't sure what happened. He turned to go. She pulled him by the coat tail. He turned back. She smiled; her lips were tucked in, mouth up at the side, chin puckered. She reached over and zipped up his pants, patted his fly-front, and said, "You can't go on out there like that," smiling like a TV housewife saying goodbye to her hubby in the morning. He wanted to say something, but it was too hot and smelly, and he didn't know what to say, and if he talked, he was sure he'd cry. He felt for the door behind him, turned the knob, and left. The giant was leaning on the wall opposite the booth door and stared at him as he came out.

He turned to leave; the little boy-girl asked if he'd like a drink, a reefer, a fix, anything to fly-on a little. But they had tempted him with drugs before and he knew where that led. It meant to be *out* because the Family wouldn't tolerate addicts. How could you depend on somebody with a habit that could betray you? He knew; he had seen it happen to his half-brother, Alonso. He jostled past and the voice became mean, a couple of octaves lower than his, asking him if he wanted to tangle. He didn't say anything but moved on. And that was when the neat, normal-looking fag had asked the first time, "What is your name?" He kept on moving. The man walked with him. They went out the door together. He was free again. The homo asked, "What's your name?"

He said, "Hinton."

154

"Pretty," the man said. "Skin like chocolate and gray eyes. Milk-chocolate Hinton."

But Hinton kept on walking, turning here and there, through the galleries, and shook the fag by going out through one of the heavy-bar, man-high turnstiles and came to stairs. A lot of distorts were there, their fix-faces weird, sitting on the staircase like they were in bleacher seats. They stared ahead as if watching some kind of performance. Hinton almost turned around to see what they were looking at. He couldn't go back, so he forced himself to go through them, and he soft-footed past and up, afraid he would step on one, or he would trip on another, or he would lose his shoe and have to grope for it, and they would drag him down and make him join them.

Then he was up and out in the street. Free. But he wasn't sure where he was. He could see he was a block from all the wild Broadway lights. He walked that way because there must be an entrance back to the subway there. The air was almost as hot outside, only it smelled of gasoline fumes instead of piss. He was a little knee-shaky. He couldn't stop perspiring. He was still hungry and thirsty. He came to 42nd Street and Broadway and turned left, into the lights. The clustered, movie and amusement lights and the crowds passing made it hotter.

He came to a food stand and the smell of frying fat made him hungry—the candy hadn't satisfied him at all. He stopped and ordered a hot dog and an orange drink. The first bite made his mouth spurt spit; his stomach contracted and churned. He had eaten nothing but candy since the morning, and then he only had a plateful of cold cooked beans at one of the Family cousin's homes. He ate the frank and sipped the orange, turning his back to and leaning his elbows on the counter. He stared out to the street through a curtain of hot lights. People walked back and forth; it didn't matter that it was late, almost four o'clock now, maybe more.

155

He watched. He had lived a few blocks away from here once, around Ninth or Tenth Avenue, but he had been too young to remember it now. His half-brother, Alonso, hung around here now. Alonso called the street no-turf. The cool cats and the hot, all the smartest cats, came here, Alonso said. Hinton couldn't see it. There were no warriors around. They all looked strange; Something Else. Small mob-fragments drifted by. Loner toughs leaned up against walls between store windows. Little handker-chiefed, short-skirted girls, tailed by hungry drifters, marched up and down in clumps, shrilling, giggling at some endless jokes. Drunks staggered, muttering, fighting their way through the heat and through their own sickness. Small explosions were going off all around; they were still celebrating here. He finished the drink and the food, but it left him unsatisfied, even hungrier. He ordered a hamburger and a grape juice. The counterman told him, "Give me the whole order at one time, will you? I can't keep trotting up and down, waiting on you all night." Hinton wished he had the heart to tell him off. Hadn't he killed his man? Didn't he have rep now? But on the other hand he remembered the tunnel and was ashamed. But who knew about that? he asked himself. He did, he told himself. Hinton ate his hamburger and drank his grape juice and thought that if the Family had been here with him, that slave wouldn't dare to talk to him like that, because they would have taken the whole operation apart and drowned the creep in his own orange juice. Yes they would. But he knew he couldn't lip the man down alone. Not yet.

Wild fag-queens with powdermask faces flutterfooted by, their feet seeming to float along the ground, tails waggling past, jackets swishing on their shaky shoulders, shirts flapping on their arses; they wore dyed hair and their eyes looked through make-up rimholes. Grinning sailors followed and you could see the make-trouble look on their faces. Weren't they just going to give it to those fruits when they caught up with them? Well,

156

Hinton didn't like homos either, and he remembered the voice that had whispered to him, inviting. That was what they turned you onto if they got hold of you.

He finished eating and walked along. He passed a newsstand. A headline said something about resumed atom-bomb testing. He passed the pokerino places where gamblers played all night. Bored boys leaned around, waiting for anything to grow into action. He knew all about that kind of waiting. In the store windows, big-headed hula-dolls waggled their electric tails; thousands of must-go-now, two-ninety-nine Swiss watches ticked out different hours; ever-thirsty birds dipped their long beaks politely and drank perpetually from glasses. Hinton thought of buying one. Great, innocent-eyed, gauze-clothed dolls blinked ahead blindly and stayed unsmirched by what their blue eyes saw. A wire coil bunched from one end back to the other while a sign said, PERPETUAL MOTION: HOW IS IT DONE? Playing cards with big-tit naked girl backs were strung in rows. He saw more ragged people, too, a lot of them—begging—and these were the most frightening because their faces were odd, distorted, and their bodies seemed badly connected. They were still horrifying even though he had heard they were all fakes.

A kid, not much younger than him, came up and asked, "Mr., you got a dime so I could have a place to sleep?" Hinton didn't answer and the kid yelled, "Well, fuck you," but not too angrily, more as if he was supposed to, and moved on. Tourists walked by, not seeing it for what it was. You could tell them by their gape-mouth look and their ever swiveling heads, and the fact that they had to see it *all* yet saw nothing at all, and that made them look crazy, too. A fat girl with orange hair beehived high walked by, offering for a price, looking satisfied with herself; that was because she was fat, Hinton thought, not like the urinal girl. Cops patrolled, club-swinging, always on the alert, but prepared only to see what was not paid for. But that was nothing

157

new, Hinton thought; that was the way it was wherever you went. And he could see the pushers passing around all kinds of dream, back and forth, and he knew that you could buy any kind of kick here, even those he had never heard or thought of. But he wasn't going to let happen to him what had happened to Alonso.

He came to the end of the block, at Ninth Avenue, turned right, crossed 42nd Street, and started back toward Broadway. He had to stop and have a few slices of pizza and a pineapple drink because the hunger had come back. He finished and walked on. He passed a lot of movie houses and looked at the titles and the photographs behind the glass cases on the walls. One place showed nudist movies all night; he wondered if he should go in. But then he might miss the Family. He passed a milk bar and went in and had a glass of milk. That didn't satisfy him and so he had a chocolate malted too. He might run out of money soon, but he couldn't help himself: He had to eat. He took out his money and started to count it. An old, slit-eyed bum gave him a hungry, no-teeth look, and he put the bread away again. He was sure he still had a lot left. His hunger kept getting worse. He walked a little further, went into a cigar store and bought a cheap cigar and some caramels. He lit the cigar, smoked it, sucked the caramel and went out to walk around some more.

He went downstairs into the subway. He passed through an amusement arcade, with a big eat-stand in the middle. He stopped and had an order of French-fries, a knish, and a papaya drink to wash it down. He left his cigar on the counter ledge beside his elbow while he ate. A jukebox played the top hits over and over again, but he couldn't make out the words over the sounds of speakers talking, trains rumbling, target shooting, game-noise, and whistling. He rocked and chewed in time to the beat. When he finished, he turned to pick up the cigar but it was missing. Someone had stolen it.

He went over to the arcade newsstand and looked at the big-breasted girls on the magazine covers, but the newsstand owner watched him suspiciously, so he bought a lot of candies, stuffing his pocket with chocolates, cashew bars, chocolate-covered raisins, candied fruits. One of the newspapers showed that someone was suing a famous actress for divorce, because of adultery, and it had a full-page picture of a beautiful blonde with an innocent smile.

He walked around the arcade looking at the games. He saw someone pass close out of the corner of his eye and turned to see a dirty-suited weird little coolie tailing him. He looked closer and saw it was himself. He recognized himself because of the pin. He stared, thinking it might be one of those distorting funny-mirrors, but it wasn't. It was because of what he had been through, the night's journey, the running, the fighting; it had made his clothes ragged and dirty. No wonder the others looked at him like he was a slave, like all the other slaves he had run across down here. He stared again, straightened himself till he saw a warrior in the mirror, a Dominator, a Family man, and he moved on.

He tried a machine gun against flashing lights that were supposed to be Jap and Kraut pilots. He fired at a light that flickered across a board which was meant to be a plane in the sky. There was a loud-speaker by his side and he heard the sound of machine guns and the dive-roar of pursuit planes, but it sounded as if it came from far away and it was unsatisfying, even though he had shot down a lot and made a high score: the gun didn't even make his hand shake. He left it and moved around the arcade, eating candies, wondering why he was still hungry. He couldn't stop eating. People hung around, giving him the hard look-over, sizing and figuring, trying to see if he was fish for their catching. He didn't dare to linger anywhere too long. He tried to keep looking cool, as cool and hard as he could, in spite of his clothes, showing that he was preyer, not prey. They eyed him and they eyed his pin. He knew the pin was a come-on, a

159

cause to fight. Everyone saw you belonged, had something, were something; it made them mad and they wanted to take it from you and make you the way they were. He couldn't take off the pin because it would reduce him to the others.

He passed a booth. Someone was standing at the end of a narrow aisle, watching him, and he turned around. The cowboy was about six feet two, wide-shouldered, and his arms were perpetually crooked into the fast-draw position. His face was young, manly, clean; the eyes were blue and innocent; the hat was tilted low over his eyes; the cowboy wore a fancy blue-checked Western shirt with white piping, a scarlet silk bandanna, a white ten-gallon hat, and the holsters on his flanks held low-slung forty-fives, big and menacing. He wore a badge. He was the sheriff.

The sheriff was set back about ten feet from a counter and a sign announced, TRY YOUR LUCK WITH THE FASTEST DRAW IN THE WEST—ONLY 10¢. There was a town painted around three sides of the sheriff; his wide stance blocked the main street. The lights from above beat down like sunlight on the nearest part of the yellow-painted town; it looked hot and Western. Behind the sheriff it was cooler, green, inviting. There was a railing in front of the booth, a coinbox on the railing, and a stiffened ammunition belt curved to step into as if you were wearing it. There were two holstered guns attached to the belt with electric wire.

Hinton thought it over while he ate a fruit bar. He could smell burning coffee; the waves of grill-heat became like the heat from sunbaked rocks, or off the hot building planks. Beyond the sheriff, it looked cool; there would be a bar there; you could get a drink and rest a long while. The figure gazed back at him; the blue eyes were lifeless, staring everywhere. If that sheriff were alive, how tough he would be, Hinton thought, how much tougher than any headbuster, in spite of the bland face.

Hinton knew all about it; he had seen The Duel, the Fair One, ever since he had been an infant. He had seen it in the movies,

160

seen it on the streets, seen it in the newsreels; they told about it in school; he had acted it out a thousand times. And it only took a dime to make the sheriff live. Of course the bullets weren't real; the risk was a fake one, Hinton told himself. But still . . . Hinton fished a dime out of his pocket and stepped into the belt. It was lowslung so he could clear the holster without trouble. He put a dime into the coinbox.

The eyes lit up. The face menaced. The sheriff lived. The lights beat down harder, making the tired scene-paint more real and unbearable, and the land the sheriff blocked more inviting. The hot lights began to make the figure of the sheriff misty, hard to see in the sunglare. The sheriff spoke; "I'm the Law of this here town and I'm here to protect it. And if you think any varmint like you is a-goin' to ride in here, a-makin' trouble, why mister, you've got another think comin', because you're a-goin' to have to get past me."

The words made Hinton angry—they were so scornfully spoken—putting him down when he hadn't even done anything.

"Now, I'm a-goin' to count to three and when I do, I want you out of this town. But if you're not gone, you just better come out firin'. You draw them pistols. You cock 'em. And when I say to fire; you fire. And we'll see who wins the showdown in three shots.

"Y'ready?" the sheriff asked and then, louder, angrier, "There's no room for your kind on the streets of El Dorado. This is a law-abidin' town and we aim to keep it that-a-way. Clear out, you polecat, or I'm a-goin' to run you in. You won't? All right then, One. Two. Three." And the sheriff's arms drew the pistols out of the holsters and moved them up and pointed them at Hinton. The eyes blazed. He looked at the two barrel circles. It was enough to make him shaky. He was almost ready to turn away; for a second he forgot to draw. "Fire," the sheriff said.

Hinton drew, cocked, but the pistols of the sheriff fired before

161

he got them halfway up. Hinton flinched and he shot. There was a sound of bullets ricocheting close.

And the sheriff's voice was saying, "Got you, you varmint. Winged you, didn't I? What? Need another lesson? Well then prepare to draw again." The arms were returning the guns to the holsters. Hinton stuffed his guns back and crouched to fire again. People were watching from the side and behind him. He paid them no mind, concentrating on his draw, looking hard, watching for the sheriff's play.

The sheriff's tough, angry eyes tried to stare Hinton down: Hinton faced up to him. The voice droned at Hinton: Hinton pressed his lips tightly. He wouldn't let himself be put down. The sheriff said, "Now." Hinton drew, cocked, shot, and hoped the bullet entered the sheriff's heart. Body would jerk back, chest would rip apart, blood of the man who put Hinton down would gush out. He heard the report of the guns. The voice of the sheriff mocked Hinton, telling him that he hadn't done it again. He had one shot left.

Hinton slid the guns into the holster. His whole body tensed now. He forgot the heat. He forgot the tiredness. He forgot his bad heel. He set his hat low on his forehead; he touched his pin; he straightened his war cigarette. He hunched his shoulders quickly once, twice, and pulled his sweaty pants free from his balls. Around him, he could see the distorted faces, the glistening eyes, hungry to see a good man put down. A fat-shouldered fairy was making remarks about him. Crazy kids, all weirds watched. He saw them out of the side of his eyes. He leaned forward. He drew at the command, cocked, and fired. Who could fast-draw better than Hinton? Bullets whistled by again and ricocheted. The mocking voice of the sheriff was telling him to get out of town, to keep on moving along. He had lost the fight.

He straightened out. His muscles were stiff from holding that tense posture. Of course. They always rigged it against you. They always put you down and you had to teach them a lesson, but good, to show them. But you couldn't do it if you did it their way. He stuck the guns back into the holsters regretfully. They felt heavy and satisfying and he was sorry to let them go. He wished they were real—then he'd show them. He reached into his pocket and took out a small box of chocolate-covered raisins and lifted his head high and poured the whole packet into his mouth. He limped slowly away, chewing his mouth clear of them.

He thought he should go back to the station platform to see if the Family had made it back. He walked around the arcade and looked at the other shooting galleries and the pinball games. Flipheads hung around; the Other hurried through, never seeing it. He passed the newsstand where he had bought all the candy. The headlines said something about a gangland-style killing. Another paper's headline said that there had been a big rumble uptown where thousands had been involved. He turned the page to read about it, but it took him too long to make out what it said. The man told him to leave the paper alone and move on if he wasn't going to buy. Hinton yawned and wondered if he should buy some more candy.

A seven-year-old kid came up to him and asked him for a dime, but he ignored the punk. He walked past a window with man-sized pictures of naked girls and he stopped to stare at them. Underneath was a pile of dusty astrology magazines, five cents apiece. His mother was always looking up her horoscope to figure out what was a good omen and what was evil any day, so she could know what she should do and what she shouldn't. Hinton put no faith in these things. Norbert, he was always saying that if he knew what the future held for him, man, what couldn't he do, what races couldn't he win. A silly dream. Hinton turned back to the naked girls, looking at their big, slick-paper breasts, shining. The kid came up again and asked Hinton to give him a dime so he could go home because he was stranded. He looked down at the kid but saw the wise, conning look; that kid didn't need any money to go home, Hinton decided: He was home—here. The kid seeing Hinton's skeptical look, said to him that he really needed the money for a drink. Hinton shook his head. The kid acted twitchy and said he needed a fix. Hinton shook his head. Then the kid looked at him, and looked up at the pin in Hinton's hat, and wanted to know if Hinton wanted to have him, because for a dollar, he would do anything Hinton wanted. Hinton was about to smack the kid, but he saw one of those wild ones looking at him, waiting for the action, and he turned away instead. He walked till he came back to the sheriff, standing under the hot lights, blocking the dusty street, waiting for Hinton.

Hinton put another dime into the slot and had another round with the sheriff and lost again. Well, he thought, drifting along out of town, it was expected—fixed. Everyone understood that. His scraped palm hurt from holding the knurled butt of the pistol. He ate some more candy and then had another hot dog and French-fries, and leaned against the counter of the stand and sipped iced tea with seven heaped teaspoons of sugar stirred into the tea, and chewed pieces of sweet candy. He looked as if he was staring at the passing people, but he was really looking over that old sheriff. No one else tried the game. That meant everyone knew it was fixed. Then he had an idea. When he finished eating he went over to try again.

Wounded Hinton, bruised Hinton, tired and drifting Hinton, Hinton the outcast, set himself against the town and its sheriff. He fought for his Family; he fought for his pin; he fought for himself. While the sheriff was sounding him and boasting and making his rep big—hadn't he put down a thousand pitiful outlaws—Hinton drew the guns and cocked them. And when the

164

word came, he fired just a fraction of a second ahead of the sheriff. This time the voice cried out in pain and told him, all right, he had won it this time. But there were two more chances and it was best out of three.

The figure stood there. Did it lean a little to the side? Did blood ooze from a hole in the shoulder, staining the front of that fancy western shirt? Did a look of pain make that impassive face a little whiter? Did it twitch? Hinton's guns were cocked and he was waiting before the word came to drawcockandfire. He won a second time because the gun leaped in his hand and it spurted fire first; hot lead sprung across the gap, and crumpled the man who had shot him down and moved him on and wouldn't let him live. Was there a new hole ripped into that flesh? The yelp of pain was joyful to Hinton and he grinned. The little kid pulled at his coat, asking him for a dime again, and he put the smoking gun down, dug, gave the kid a dime, and got ready for the third shot. He won that one too; he got the sucker right in the eyeball.

Hinton, very tired, straightened slowly in spite of his wounds, sucked in air, and felt new now—a man. He had faced up to and beaten the sheriff. He could have won another round, but he had the sense to put the guns away now, even though he was entitled to a free fight. He turned and walked away, began to strut through the arcade, and out; it was time to go and see if the Family had made it back.

The fag sounded him one more time and he wondered if he shouldn't go with the fag and have a kick or two and then deck the fag and take his money. But the fag was no slender boy himself, but big enough, able to take care of himself, and that simpering, pleading look ambushed something hard. He moved on, paid another token, and went down to the station. A couple leaned in a corner; he couldn't tell if they were men or women, but they were shielded by a spread-out raincoat and doing something. People passing didn't stop them. A transit bull standing nearby didn't see a thing.

When he got there, Dewey and The Junior had come and were looking around nervously, ready to cut out. They wanted to know where the others were. He didn't know; everyone had been separated. He told them that they would make it home by the next Coney Island train. They looked a little uncomfortable, as if they were deserting, but they were really glad enough to go. He gave them the order feeling good now, feeling strong, and they took his command because that took the responsibility away from them. They sensed his new strength now and they were under *him* now, even though Dewey was Hinton's elder brother.

When their train came, they got on, sat down. Hinton almost fell asleep. The Junior opened his comic book, but his eyes kept shutting as—though he had read it before—he tried to begin again.

July 5th, 4:30—5:20 A.M.

It was only a matter of coasting home. Exhaustion relaxed them. But two more things happened on the way home.

The train, as always at this hour, was slow. It had gotten well into Brooklyn. Dewey, sitting between Hinton and The Junior, fell asleep. They sat in a corner, under one of those DOES SHE OR DOESN'T SHE ads, where a young, beautiful woman leans over a little boy, almost kissing him on the mouth. The ad says it's about hair dye. The Family always had fun with that one.

Hinton kept dozing off. The Junior was blearily reading again, the part about where the big battle had taken place in front of Babylon and the leader of the Rebel army had been slain and the Greek heroes were trying to decide what they would do now. Two couples got on the train, blond-hair crew-cuts and their doll-

167

eyed girls. They were wearing fancy evening clothes as if they had just come from a dance—a prom maybe. They were big boys, football-player types, and they gave the three men a hard look even though they hadn't done anything. Hinton half-saw and woke up to those cold, contemptuous stares. What right did those squares have to look at them that way? What had the Family done to them? They were minding their own business, weren't they?

The couples sat opposite them. The girls put their heads on the boy's shoulders and closed their eyes. The boys kept staring at the tired warriors, watching them warily, ready for anything. Why, Hinton wondered? They didn't mean anything. All he could think of now was sleeping.

Hinton looked at the girls from under almost closed lids. They were clean looking, innocent, ideal teen-ager types about to be pretty young women, the kind you saw on television all the time and dreamed about. Now and then he even saw this kind at school, but not too often. One of them was blonde; her nose was slender-bridged and upturned a little, pulling her lip up. Her long legs were primly pressed together. She looked very clean. It would be nice to have a girl. It would be nice to cut out from the Family, to retire from bopping. Hinton felt wearier. Maybe he could get a girl, not exactly like this one—blonde, yet not really blonde; white, but not white—light-colored, long-haired. She would be innocent, sweet, from some other part of town, dressed clean, beautiful, slender—go steady—marry—a family. He would have a job, a chance. Having someone like her to marry would give him ambition. They would have a home and a dog. He would rise in the world and he would become—he wasn't sure what. Something behind a desk: an executive. It would involve ordering men around because he would be a big man, a very big man, and he wouldn't have to do it by bopping. He'd say "Do this. Call him. I'll buy that. I'll sign the contract," and

168

talk into an intercom to Miss. . . . They'd all bow to him and he'd control, like the gangsters did these days, in a clean way: no violence. He half-dreamed about that.

The dream became more commanding and his eyes were staring but he hardly saw the couples across the way. Dewey had slipped down and his head was lying on Hinton's shoulder. Hinton saw the advertisement by the side of his head. Her face was lovely, sweet and young, unattainable too, a dream-mother. His hand reached up and he stroked the picture, following her cheek and chin line tenderly, his fingertips feeling it like it was almost flesh, not paper. He sighed, leaned back, and looked. He saw those two prom cats looking at him, half-grinning. He didn't look back at them because then he'd have to recognize what their stare meant, and he'd have to challenge them, and that would lead to a little back and forth jive, and none of the Family were packed. These days you couldn't tell even about prom cats. Everyone packed a little two- or three-inch slice. Everyone knew that. They didn't laugh openly at him so he relaxed and pretended to sleep and soon, after five or six stops, they got off. As they left they turned and gave the Family the put-down look, but he pretended not to see it. And he knew now that he'd never have this dream; not that way. So he'd get it another way, he thought. Well, fuck those motherfuckers, he thought. Avenue J. He would remember that station and someday, just someday, he might lead the men and come down on a little raid around here, looking for them, because who were they to jive the Family?

It rankled him and he couldn't sleep. The Junior's eyes kept shutting, his head nodding over his comic book. Hinton had to jump up; the anger wouldn't let him rest. His shoulder bounced Dewey's head. They stared at him. He walked up and down the empty train aisle. He should have challenged those coolie bastards.

When they got to their stop they got off. They had a few

blocks to walk through Colonial Lord Turf. It was almost dawn; no one would be awake at this time. Hinton wondered if the Lord's plenipos had gotten back from the great conference. The others trudged sleepily, but the hatred made Hinton bounce. He wanted to do *something*. Then he got the great idea.

He shook The Junior and he nudged Dewey and told them, pointing to the cigarette in their hat-bands, "We're a war party and we finish like a war party, you hear now? We've got to make one last raid."

"Man, *you* make a raid. I'm tired, man. I'm too tired," Dewey whined.

The Junior just looked at Hinton, stupefied. Hinton told them, "Man, we've just got to do it or we lose our self-respect."

"Now? We've been up all night. You're losing your mind. You're flipping. You're becoming something else, like that Willie, man."

But Hinton began to talk, reminding them that they had lost the core part of their army. The enemy would know it and they would come, bopping, japping, rumbling down on them, raiding them silly, unless the Family struck first and showed them, but good. *Now. Now!* As a defensive action. The Family was tougher than they thought, *more* tough than before. Who did those mothers think they were? The Family would come down on them and clean them up once and for all, but good, but the best. Would they be expecting it? Dewey tried to argue against it, but Hinton was getting himself more and more excited with the idea and the anger carried him along and his fury began to wake up Dewey and The Junior. Hinton rehearsed the old slights, foresaw insults to come, reminded them of traditional territorial fights, predicted what would happen and how a raid would give them much rep for big heart. All this part of the world would *know,* and all the other gangs would have respect and would come around and want to ally with the Dominators.

170

They *had* to do it, once and for all. But best of all, it would be totally unexpected.

"But man, what about the truce?" Dewey asked.

"That truce means shit, man, shit, and you know it. After it broke, up there, it means shit, and it's every army for himself and we have got to make it now. *Now!* I mean tomorrow will be too late."

And he had them worked into a trot now and they were going along fast. They tore off two antennas from cars for whips as they passed; they found a thrown-out chair and took it apart to use one of the screw-head legs as a club. They swept down into the heart land of the Colonial Lords.

Most of the Colonial Lords lived in a housing project. The Family charged down in the dim dawn light, looking for a Lord or two, or for one of their women, but no one was there. While the others japped in the playground, The Junior behind a jungle gym and Dewey in a kiddie pipe, Hinton came out into the middle of the project. He stood on a lawn, in the center of a vast circle of eight fourteen-story apartment houses which towered above him. The First of the Colonial Lords lived in one of them. Yelling, Hinton dared him to come down, and dared him to Fair-Fight man to man, and insulted everyone connected with him, allies as well as personal family. Hinton's voice rang out, high, going far along the slowly brightening areas, and beat up against the huge houses where it echoed back, faint, higher, ringing. No one came. The quieter it was, the louder Hinton screamed. But nothing moved. Nothing at all. He kept this up for a while and he could tell that The Junior and Dewey had big respect for him. He had made his rep. He swaggered away and they strutted behind him over to the handball courts.

Hinton took out his Magic Marker. The Colonial Lords had written their marks all over that ball-wall. Hinton wrote that the Dominators had come down LAMF and they shit on the Colonial Lords, whose mothers were, one and all, whores. And there was not one man among the Lords who was not a bastard. And then, while Dewey and The Junior supported him on their shoulders, he drew a picture, high, high up. He did it well, using a few lines, but showing it all, because wasn't he the Family artist? He drew a picture of a woman in oral intercourse with a man. He titled the man, Father of the Dominators; and he titled the woman, Mother of the Lords. And then, on one side, he drew a portrait of a woman being raped by a huge-organed giant and he titled the man The Dominators, and he titled the woman Debs of the Lords. He took great care to make the woman's face very ugly and he wrote down as many of the Lords' girls' names as he could remember. And then he drew a lot of tiny little men standing around and watching, their tongues hanging out. And he called the little men, The Lords.

Then he called a charge. They began running through the project streets, swinging the antenna whips and the club, making trumpet sounds, sounding the Lords again, daring them to come out and fight, trampling all over their sacred turf.

No one came out. Hinton's throat hurt. He gave the order to march away. They jived along, out of that land.

July 5th, 5:20—6:00 A.M.

Before going home, Hinton led The Junior and Dewey down
the street toward the beach. They followed him; he had become
the Father. The morning wind was coming at them from the sea.
It was still hot, but every step took them into cooler and cooler
areas. It was lighter above the housetops, but still dark below.

They walked toward the boardwalk. When they came to the
last block, Hinton halted them before crossing the street. He
stood, hand raised, looking up and down. Nothing there but a
garbage truck, grinding refuse, yellower than the murky light
coming down from the overcast sunrise. The street lights were
paling; they had blue, fluorescent edges. Hinton waved his hand
the way patrol leaders did; they crossed the street, walking cool,
alert for surprises. Far up the street a Headbuster patrolled, his

173

back toward them. They were on their territory now; everything had a tremendous and comforting familiarity. They knew it to its confines, six short blocks by four long blocks. They could cover it in a short time—each brick was completely known, each stain, each sign, each gunmark on the concrete sidewalks, each hiding place. It was like knowing an endless and soul-freeing space where there could be no real threat. There wasn't as much space in the rest of the whole city. They drank it all in, everything from the cracked asphalt to the strutty rise of the roller coaster over the houses. It was there. There. Comforting after their night. They began to walk along the last block before coming to the boardwalk.

Hinton smelled the cool sea wind and began to feel a joyful excitement and quickened his step again. The boys moved a little faster. Hinton began to trot. They trotted after him. He began to shout, shouting nothing, letting the choking in his throat find a wordless opening. He began to run. They ran after him, laughing, silly, unable to control themselves. Was this all there was to being a man, Hinton wondered as he ran? Was this the way you became a leader, a Father? He ran up the ramp to the boardwalk. They ran after him; their feet clattered on the wood, keeping time. A few people strolled along the empty stretch of wooden walk which disappeared along both sides, fading into the morning's red haze. A few fishermen were arriving for early surf fishing. Farther off, a family loaded with blankets and beach equipment crossed the boardwalk, coming to the beach early. The morning sun was balled red in the haze, hanging off to the right. The littered sand and the red-stained water, placid under the wind, lay ahead.

Hinton pointed and yelled, "The Ocean!"

They yelled, "The Ocean, The Ocean!" and they all laughed hysterically.

Hinton ran down the stairs to the sand and all the way down

174

the beach to the water, veered off sharply to the left, slipping, touching the soft surge of the wave, and feeling the wetness coming in through the rips in his shoe. It was chill-shocking, burning on his abrasions, and then cooling and pleasant. He dipped his scraped hand into the water and shook loose drops into the air.

They ran. They couldn't stop laughing now, trying hard to keep the joy from degenerating into baby giggles. They cackled and made howling, shrieky sounds. A few gulls flew up at their approach; wind blew scraps of paper lightly, lifting them; sand grains sprayed upward as their running feet hit the beach. The wind from the sea was cooling now, almost chilling, and all the air that had stifled them the whole night seemed to be clearing away, and it was as if they were coming loose from a palpable thickness now; every step they took was lighter and they felt hilariously lifted off the ground until they barely felt their exhaustion. Hinton no longer cared that the ruination of his fancy Italian-style shoes that had begun in the park—how far away that seemed, as if it hadn't even happened that day or that week or ever, really—was almost complete now. Where was he going to get another fifteen bucks for shoes like these? It didn't matter. It didn't matter at all.

Dewey did a cartwheel, the pin in his hat glittering in a circle. The Junior tried it and the war cigarette fell out of his hat. He picked it up and was about to stick it back into the band of his hat when he had an idea. He turned and ran to Hinton, kneeled, and gave it to him. Hinton took it, held it for a second, and put it into his mouth. The Junior lit it for him. Hinton puffed it once, twice, hard and cool, and then let the smoke dribble out of his mouth and nose to be caught, whipped away, and feathered into nothing by the sea wind. He pinched out the cigarette and stuck it back into The Junior's hatband. Dewey looked on and nodded. Then Dewey and The Junior took out the war cigarettes from their hatbands and gave them to Hinton who put them into a half-empty pack of his own. The war party was over. Hinton turned and began to walk back to the Boardwalk. The others followed. It was understood. Hinton was now Father.

They walked down the beach for a few blocks. They turned in toward the land and began to walk home. It was close to six o'clock now and it was completely light on the beach. The shadows were still hard and dark in the streets. The seawind blew warm dirt up from the streets. Here the wind smelled of salt, rank weeds, picking up the smells of decaying houses, sour old wood, carrying the garbagy smells of concession-refuse inland.

They walked till they came to the candy store where they always met. Some girls were sitting there, perched on the newsbox. They had been waiting all night—Hector's woman, Bimbo's woman, Dewey's woman, and The Junior's woman. They talked and the daughters told them that Arnold had made it back hours ago. Arnold had told them all about it and that Ismael had just disappeared. No one knew what had happened to him. They told Hector and Bimbo's women as much as they knew about their men. The girls nodded, kept their faces cool, lit cigarettes, and blew smoke out of their noses. They shook hands all around and parted. Bimbo's woman began to weep; Hector's girl put her arm around her, holding her, as they walked away. Dewey and The Junior went off with their women, arms around one another. Hinton waited till everyone was out of sight and walked toward The Prison.

Both sides of the street were still in morning shadow. A lot of the houses here were old and wooden, unpainted clapboard, leaning, supported by the fact that they were up against one another. He wasn't going to be the Father after all, Hinton thought, not unless he wanted to duel Arnold for it. He could see himself putting Arnold down, for hadn't he gotten his man and hadn't he led a raid? He wished he had a girl to wait for him like the others had. A girl would watch him man-to-man with Arnold, like he had fought the sheriff. She would fall in love with him. He thought again of a vague girl. He saw himself winning her, going with her, like the others. He saw himself having sex with her. He didn't think of it so much in excitable terms; somehow it was . . . clean . . . dignified. But if he got a woman, he knew he wouldn't really care about being the Father because if you had what you wanted, what was the point of fighting? It wasn't worth it. At least now he had won his rep, and now they knew him to be a man who could lead, even if he did not always choose to fight—certainly not for the leadership of the Family. For hadn't he brought the remnant home? Arnold hadn't done that, and Hector, Bimbo, Lunkface, they hadn't been able to do that either. It would be enough to be a big man of the turf and get, perhaps, an Uncleship. Then he should be able to get a steady girl instead of having to take the kind of girls everyone made it with.

He came to The Prison. It was a four-story brick apartment house. They lived on the top floor. Their apartment had been found for them, as always, by the Department of Welfare, and it was the twentieth place he had lived since he had been born, or five more places than he was old. Most of the hallway lights were out. The stairs leaned free from the walls; Alonso called them free-floating. He stopped inside the front door and listened. They must have caught Hector, Bimbo, and Lunkface who might have talked; they might have sent cops to wait for him. He heard nothing except for the crazy old Jew-lady moving around on the ground floor. But then, she never seemed to sleep, always muttering to herself—a witch. You had to look out for her because she had a glass eye and a claw hand and she said wild words. Some, like his mother, said she could hex you, but he didn't believe in things like that.

He waited. He heard nothing. He took the chance and began to walk up the stairs. He was all fagged out. The only sound was the creaking of those prison steps—hard to walk up.

The top floor had four apartments, two left and two right,

facing one another. There were two toilets in the center, one for every two apartments. Before going into his house, he went to the toilet. He always shit half-standing, never willing to sit on the seat, but today he couldn't do it. Too tired. The walls, though it was still too dark to see, were covered with inscriptions, and in the time they had lived there, he, his brothers, his sisters, had all added their words. Roaches froze on the walls. The sound of his piss falling into the toilet was loud, but familiar, and comforting. He could feel the sense of relaxation working its way around his body from his emptying insides. He leaned his head against the wall to the side and almost fell asleep. When he had finished, he went into the cell.

There was no light bulb at that end of the hall. He lit a match. On the wall, next to his door, he wrote "Fuck Norbert," at the bottom of a long list of Fuck Norberts. He opened the door. The door opened directly into the kitchen. There was a little room off to his right. It was dark there. Three of his younger brothers and a younger sister slept there; no one moved in the blackness. In the kitchen there was a pile of clothes on the floor, some pans of cooked, now cold food were on the stove, a few empty beer cans lay around, there were some half-filled food cans his mother had forgotten to put away, and unwashed dishes were on the table and the sink-shelf and in the sink. He went through the kitchen. As he moved through the hot, unmoving air, flies rose. The baby lay in a crib on wheels and was crying rhythmically. Hinton rocked the crib once, twice, and went on through.

The next room was a dining room-bedroom. A little light came through the open door from the front room. His mother, Minnie, fat, perspiring in the stifling sweat and baby-pissed air, was being fucked by her man, Norbert, who had been living with them, on and off, for about two years now. As Hinton passed through their faces looked in his direction and though their eyes

178

were wide open, they didn't seem to see him at all, only glared in his direction. Minnie's fat, round face was full of pleasure, only she looked like she was being tortured and she made little shriek-grunt sounds. Norbert's face was round too, but Hinton didn't see it clearly; Hinton knew that Norbert's lips were curled back and he was grinning, but it wasn't really a smile. Norbert made panting sounds like exhorting a horse to come on in. The bed made a creaking, monotonous, pleasure-sound.

"Get out of here or I'll clout you," Norbert said, but he said that all the time anyway.

"Where you been? I been worried sick," Minnie said and shrieked and frowned and closed her eyes and moaned.

Hinton went into the back room. It was lighter here. The light and dust on the windows opaqued the morning into one steady sheet of gray light. Alonso and his older sister were in the opened couch-bed together. Alonso hadn't been home in two weeks now. They were lying there, naked, with only a sheet to cover them. She slept on her back with her mouth open and the bottoms of her eyes open, but not seeing. Alonso's hollow cheek was propped up on his hand and he was staring into the darkness where his Mother and Norbert were making it. His other hand drooped over the side of the bed and his fingers were propped on his bongo because Alonso never moved without his bongo to give him the beat. His fingers kept time to the bed-creak. Hinton looked down at Alonso and heard the bed-creak, baby-wail, Norbert-pant, shriek, and soft thump of the bongo again and again. Alonso didn't look at Hinton at all, but his skinny face had that smile that made you have to hate him; the smile that told you that he knew the answers, had seen it all, and anything you did was foolish, too childish for words. Well, what did you expect of a junkie, Hinton thought meanly.

But, unable to stop the excitement of having to show Alonso what he had done that night, he said, "Man, you know what

179

happened tonight? You know where I've been? You know what I did?" And Hinton squatted beside the bongo, close to Alonso to tell him.

"That Minnie. That Norbert. Tick tock. Predictable," Alonso said.

Hinton began to tell about his night.

"Jim, you been playing soldier. When will you learn? When are you going to stop that bopping and, you know, punk stuff?"

And Hinton, as he had so many times, tried to tell Alonso about the Family and what it meant, and how they had gone through so much that night.

But Alonso kept smiling that smile and nothing made any sense with that smile looking you in the face. "Jim, don't tell me that, you know, brother-shit. I have been through it all. Take, you know, advice. There is only one thing and that is the kick, the Now. Nothing else counts. Get yours. Get it because, you know, no one cares and they will always put you down in the end, Jim, and the only word that counts is, you know, Now. Not that foolish brother and bopping jazz, Jim. Now. Because if it all don't go up in any, you know, twenty minutes; up, all gone; then they are going to put you down and keep you down. Now."

It was an old argument. Hinton couldn't argue about it. He couldn't tell Alonso that he was a junkie and alone and that was a terrible way to be and so couldn't understand what it meant to have a Family. But Alonso smiled that what-do-you-know-about-it smile, and against that look, nothing could prevail. But Hinton told it anyway. Alonso's fingers kept the time beats. Hinton watched a bubble of spit on the corner of his sister's lips and beads of sweat rolling down her breasts to the cleft. And when he had finished, the smile hadn't changed one bit and Hinton was sure Alonso's scorn was boundless.

He stood up. The baby was still crying, but Norbert and Minnie had finished. Hinton went back through their room and into

180

the kitchen. He shook the crib. The baby stopped crying for a second. He looked around and went over to a pan on the stove; there were a few French fries left in it. He took one and brought it over and put it in the baby's mouth. It stopped yelling and began to suck. He went back through Minnie's room. They were lying, fat cheeks pressed together, smiling, and the light gave them a sweet cherubic look now, as they rested up for the next jazzing. He went back past Alonso's smile and around the bed and he opened the window and climbed out onto the fire escape and sat down, his back against the wall.

He could see far down the alleyway behind the housebacks. The light was hot, thick, uniform, and poured down like something boiling into the spaces between the houses. The back-yard trees hung limp and hot, their leaves dusty. Hinton's knees drew up tighter, tighter, till his whole body was pressed tightly together and he clasped his shins tightly and his head was pressed into his kneetops, and his eyes stared out over the trees and through the laundry lines toward where the sea would be if it wasn't blocked off by a big hotel.

And after a while, he lay down on his side, his head on his crumpled hat, and kept curled up there, staring, his thumb in his mouth, till he fell asleep.

How I Came to Write *The Warriors* and What Happened After

Sol Yurick

It's hard to remember when the idea for *The Warriors* first hit me. All memory, even when there are hard records, is tricky. When trying to recollect and reconstruct the fragments of memory, time sequences become scrambled; effects are substituted for causes; events that occurred in sequence seem to have happened at the same time. Of the fragile bio-chemical-electrical basis of memory storage, who can really say?

I think I read Xenephon's *The Anabasis* when I was in college (1945, after I got out of the army, until about 1951). Originally, I wanted to be a scientist but I finally had to accept that I had no aptitude for mathematics. I gravitated to psychology but found that I couldn't believe in anyone's theories. I switched and majored in literature with a philosophy minor. As I read the philosophical texts,

I began to regard philosophers with suspicion. What they talked about, I didn't see in the world around me. For instance it seemed to me that Socrates, in *The Republic*, never answered Thrasymachus's might-makes-right proposal: therefore all philosophy stopped waiting for an answer.

The Warriors replicates the journey in *The Anabasis*. I didn't read Xenephon's book—the Penguin edition; translation by Rex Warner, titled *The Persian Expedition* . . . or was it called *The March Upcountry?*—for any course, although I did begin Homeric Greek but dropped out after a month or so. One might note, and perhaps it isn't, on a deep political-psychological level, that *The Anabasis* took place in what is now Iraq, where "Western Civilization" is taking another defeat.

It was sometime during my college years, influenced by my first encounters with the great books of Western literature, that I decided I wanted to become a writer. My literary heroes of those years were Kafka, Dostoyevsky, and Joyce, later to be replaced by Proust. The New Criticism was becoming the dominant mode of literary analysis. This theory discouraged reading any work with reference to biography, history, politics, or culture. Critics were enjoined to treat the work as a self-enclosed, aesthetic object which, if it was great—or made great by a cabal of celebrators—always reflected something called "The Human Condition." (It was the conceit of the time to think that this "Human Condition" was the same everywhere and everywhen, a point disputed by post-modernists.) Psychoanalysis and its heretical variants were beginning to become democratized, permeating all (well, at least the middle class) sectors of society; most of the leading critics of the time were Freudian. The Sartrean version of existentialism (absurdism and the tragic condition of Man—we didn't speak of Woman in those days— tragic because Man was condemned to death) became, along with its opposite, logical positivism, the fashionable philosophies in dialectical conflict. No one dared speak of Marxism in those early

Cold War years. What psychoanalysis, existentialism, and the New Criticism had in common was the emphasis on individualism.

The Cold War influenced *all* fields of discourse. Unbeknownst to me, the great canon of Western literature was used as a tool in the propaganda war against Soviet-style communism with its socialist realism and contempt for the now historically outmoded, great "bourgeois" canon of literature, and the "decadent formalism" of modernism (read Eliot and Joyce, for instance).

One of the great acts of faith of the time was that the creative artist was seriously neurotic. In fact it was supposed to be dysfunction that fueled the artist's ability to create. Of those who didn't create, "ordinary" people who were psychotic or neurotic, we didn't speak; neurosis was still, in those days, an elite condition.

It was in this climate that I decided to become a writer. I had discovered, writing term papers, that I had a natural aptitude for creative and imaginative writing. This was odd; I didn't speak English for the first five years of my life. Later, as soon as I began elementary school, I became a compulsive reader (by high school I was reading four books a week beside my schoolwork).

I wanted to be a serious, perhaps avant garde writer. I disdained popular culture, although I read popular material (such as comics and science fiction, which was not regarded seriously in those days) and loved the movies. At first I wrote poetry, then later short stories and novels. In those days the mythology had it that you began with short stories and graduated to novels. My exposure and attraction to modernist experimentalism not withstanding, I also believed in "the story," the narrative bound—no matter what games you played with text—by the reality that takes the human through space, time, and society toward death, a reality in which events occur in sequence. I was, being young, naive about what it took to become a serious writer. I believed that talent alone would ultimately succeed. At the same time I secretly wondered if reputation wasn't also to some extent a function of promotional propaganda (which I consider the

185

discipline(s) of aesthetics to be) that made the "great" work. It seemed as if "serious" analysis by "serious" critics, using properly obscurantist jargon turned the work into a commodity that would allow for a working class of meaning-miners to forever uncover layer after layer of hidden meaning and elevate the silliest of works into objects of worshipful greatness. (Years later I was to read Schucking's *The Sociology of Literary Taste*, which confirmed my suspicions. And even later on I was to discover our State's—the omnipresent CIA [it made the reputation of Pasternak's *Dr. Zhivago*, really a second-rate book, for instance, and funded prestigious literary magazines] among other agencies—interest in literature. But that's another story.)

Skip ahead a few years; it's sometime in the period of 1950–55; I was writing and submitting short stories and writing novels. The stories were regularly rejected. In order to stay alive, I had gone to work for what was then known as the Department of Welfare of N.Y.C. I came in contact with, as it were, the lower social and economic depths . . . impoverished families, culturally and racially different. I went through a kind of social shock. I had grown up in poverty during the Great Depression. My own family had been preserved from disaster during the Great Depression of the '30s by receiving welfare checks. But the difference between my clients and my parents' generation was huge. My parents were communists. They thought of themselves as the coming elite of the world, in fact even a new and superior species, the Proletariat. History was supposed to be on their side. They fought and organized. My clients did not. I couldn't understand why. If you were poor and society was against you, you either fought politically or became a crook, as a loan shark, who had considered the options during the Depression, told me. What other choice was there? I was later to understand the complex reasons that led to what seemed their passivity.

Some of the children of these families were what was then called

Juvenile Delinquents. Many of them belonged to fighting gangs. Some of these gangs numbered in the hundreds; they were veritable armies. This social phenomenon was viewed, on the one hand, as the invasion of the barbarians, only this time they came from the inside rather than from the outside. On the other hand, there was something subversive about the gangs (and especially the music that they loved . . . rock). The social thinkers, academic and popular, failed to understand why these social formations of the deprived crystallized in the midst of what we were told again and again were economically good times.

The media inflated the gang phenomenon to mythic proportions. (Of course they spoke of the "lower" classes: of the existence of violent middle-class gangs, nothing was said.) But then the media deals in the commodification of fear, alarm, and scandal. *The New York Times* ran a multipart series. What seemed like a national eruption of juvenile gangism also gave rise to a publication and theatrical industry. Books proliferated: *Rebel Without a Cause* (the title, and contents of this book almost implied that if the rebel had a "cause" there would not be rebelliousness but possibly rebellion), *The Blackboard Jungle*, *The Amboy Dukes*, etc. A famous killing in New York led to a theatrical production (actually two; Paul Simon's spectacular failure being the second), *West Side Story* (Capeman, Salvatore Agron, meets *Romeo and Juliet*; trivial and silly), and Warren Miller's *The Cool World*. The academy produced a mass of sociological and psychological studies.

I think the elements for *The Warriors* began to come together sometimes during the '50s. I was having a talk with a friend of mine, a writer whose mother and father had been successful Hollywood script writers. He was trying to explain to me what constituted a good idea (the "high concept") for a script. Almost as a joke, I hit upon the notion of a story of a fighting gang based on, or paralleling, the course of *The Anabasis*. Once uttered, I dropped the idea. I thought the notion was ingenious, but not really serious. Yet I didn't forget it.

187

Again I pass over the years. I got married, quit working for the Department of Welfare. My wife, Adrienne, told me to quit work and go back to school or stay home and write. I decided to go to graduate school (1959–61), Brooklyn College, so that I could become a teacher while I continued to write. At this point I had completed two and a half novels . . . that would never be published.

This is a diversion, yet to the point, for it entails how I moved away from the influence of my college readings. While I was going to graduate school, my first short story was published in a short-lived literary journal: *The Noble Savage*. Publication hardened my resolve to be a full-time writer rather than a teacher. I was given permission to write a novel as a master's thesis. This became *Fertig*, which played a critical role in my development as a writer and, indirectly, in the formation of *The Warriors*.

Originally, when I began to conceive the idea for *Fertig*, I was under the influence of the existentialists, particularly Camus. At first I had wanted to write a spare, perhaps puzzling, Camusian novel like *The Stranger*, with a touch of Kafka. This book attempts to picture a man not so much against his society as outside it (as I thought I was temperamentally). In part, what Camus had tried to do was to strip away the surrounding social and material conditions, isolating his character and his act from contaminating culture, time and place.

When we first meet Meursault (the Stranger), his mother has just died. He seems emotionally unaffected. Then he commits what appears to be a random murder, a murder without understandable motives . . . in fact, seemingly without motive at all. He is condemned by a horrified court. The court partly bases its horror on Mersault's "inhuman" disregard for his mother's death. This disregard not only denies one of the fundamental tenets of bourgeois society but its Freudian variant. We, in this country, would ask if he was a psycho- and/or sociopath. Camus didn't use any of these

188

categories. (At that point in time, in the late '40s and through the '50s, the question of random and/or serial killers, whose psychology was, and still remains, a complete puzzle, had not yet been shown to be not uncommon.) I wanted my protagonist, Fertig, to commit such a crime.

Now the insane person (or, these days, the one thought to be missing the proper responsibility-gene) is neither for or against the society in which he or she lives but is, nevertheless, a disturbance to it . . . a disturbance that must be accounted for. Our society, America in particular, has found it hard to deal with what appears to be the nonrational. What our thinkers resort to is to shift the inexplicable into one or another psychological and/or sociological categories, thus solving the problem of the irrational person, and so negating his or her act. However, what of the rational person who commits horrendous crimes (such as those who work for the State's interrogation bureaus, and assassinators)? The actions of the intelligent, rationally antirational man may be the greatest danger.

One could read Mersault's motivation one of two ways—as a totally random act of a man without reason and/or as protest . . . but against what? The system, whatever it was? (Now it should be understood that while this "protest," if that was what it was, against bourgeois life was neither politically left nor right in the usual sense. Nor was Mersault's act criminal in the usual sense, which in most cases implies reason. So the question remains: protest against what? Camus never made that clear.

But had Camus really succeeded in detaching himself from his background and its traditions? The place was Algiers, the time may or may not have been immediately before or after World War II. This culture, in which Camus had grown up, was French-colonized Algeria. (Camus was later to say, in the midst of the Algerian liberation struggle, that Algeria *was his mother*. What's more, Mersault's victim was an Arab. One can speculate; if Meursault had killed the Arab because of social, political, or class differences, the

189

court might have understood. That is to say, if Meursault had socially shared motives for killing the Arab, he was not a threat to the social order. Conversely, if Mersault was sane, which is to say rational (rationality always defined in terms of what a society calls rational), and did this irrational act, then he was a threat to social order because who knew where and against whom he might strike next.

(What has all this to do with *The Warriors*? Remember that gangs were thought to be an irrational manifestation.)

What Camus was trying to get at was that there are empty interstices of understanding between one action and another action, a gap that is the ground of artistic, philosophic, and scientific creation.

Further, even though Camus had tried to detach his hero from culture and tradition, I began to find, as I read more, disguised literary references—such as *The Divine Comedy* . . . particularly "Paradiso"—in *The Stranger*. What this said to me was that in spite of his attempt to escape the constraints of Western tradition into— what? pure anomie?—he was bound by it. That is to say that Camus's subtext denied his philosophical endeavor. He could not imagine the mind of the truly random killer. All this is by way of saying that you cannot go from the pure universal to the particular because, whether you like it or not, you always construct the universal out of the particular, sabotaging the universal.

Perhaps, for Camus the killing represented his *unconscious* reaction to the Algerian liberation forces. I was not aware of the subtext when I first read the book . . . until the '60s.

So, as I was writing my book and as I thought I was drawn to this existentialist philosophy, perhaps because of my own psychological makeup and my commitment to reason—negated, of course, as it is for all creative writers, by my practice that favored quantum leaps of understanding and construction—and because of my experience as a social welfare worker, I began to be forced to begin looking for new ways to express the real world in my writing. That is to say, I sought, and had to invent a rational motive for my hero's crime. At the same time this *real* (I don't care what the postmodernist relativists have to say) world was more irrational and absurd than the existentialist philosophers—those meta-hyper-rationalists—could imagine. In order to try to understand how my hero would encounter this "real" world, and move through it, I began readings in practical and theoretical sociology, anthropology, and psychology (I rejected Freudian and Jungian thought, or any variant thereof. On the other hand, I found that behaviorism was mechanistically Laplacian). The sociologists who interested me the most were Weber and Durkheim, perhaps because of their interest in the "primitive" and the ancient (read prerational). For what were my clients, I must have thought, but prerational? And what were the fighting gangs but prerational? Slowly, even without knowing it, I thought I had begun to form aspects of a theory of writing based on *my* sociology.

And yet, at the same time, as I hunted for the rational behind the mysterious apparent and irrational immediate surface, the ordinary, the non- or antiliterary, I began to discern that even behind that, negating the whole social and psychological quasi-scientific endeavor that sought to explain why humans did what they did, lurked the ever-recurrent presence of the ritualistic, ceremonial, and mythic (which meant to me the unresolved "primitive") in everyday life. Why? As I observed life, ordinary people, in twentieth-century U.S.A., suddenly became as exotic and "primitive" to me as, say, Australian aborigines. And, reflexively, slowly I began to see that the mythic and metaphysical and *something biological* (the urge to form tribal/family-like/gang groups in any and every culture, so-called primitive or modern sophisticated so-called civilized in history) also played a role in the discipline of sociology-aspiring-to-be-hard-science (as later I was to discover the haunting, left-over "background radiation" of metaphysics in science and mathematics).

191

I came to see my mistake in being drawn to existentialist thought. To escape the spell of Camus's creature, I reached back into the memories of my early life and found that I had distinct, *rational*, formable, statable grievances against the system of our country. I and my family had suffered what to me was perhaps the greatest nonphilosophical, nonpsychoanalytic, materialist, if you will, *traumatic* absurdity . . . the Depression of the '30s. My parents were communists. Coming from a communist background and being a Jew added to my sense of alienation from American life. These social and economic traumas had become part of my unconscious. To me, being a writer was like being a rebel. I'll show you what your world is really like, I must have thought. And what of the gangs? Theirs, too, was a form of revolt. Some gangs take to the streets; some gangs emerge in October 1917.

And the more I thought about it, given our social system (even at that time), the more I saw the social forces as they "really" were. I couldn't allow myself to present my stories in the kind of semidreamlike ways that Camus and Kafka used. To put it in a kind of old-fashioned quasi-Marxist terminology (which I would not have done when I was writing *Fertig*), the attempt to reconcile the multiple conflict of multiple interests (there are always 613 contradictions) was what constituted the concrete basis of irrationality in everyday life. I knew. I had, after all, been a bureaucrat. I had learned what went into the making of what appeared to outsiders as systemic absurdity in government; that if you went back into the making of every regulation and law, there was a kind of ancient craziness, a craziness embodied in the very flesh. And more, I knew, unlike the postmodernist, academic glossolalists, that difficult-to-understand writing is, in fact, a government and business strategy . . . in order how, as Dickens put it, not-to-do-it, or prevent it from being done as long as possible, or to do it before anyone understood what was being done.

At the time I was writing *Fertig*, the emerging dominant psychosocial theory of the day had it that anyone who murdered was psychotic and so not responsible for their acts. (This theory didn't, of course, take into account those who killed for gain—Mafia, for instance—or for reasons of state that involved soldiers and CIA operatives, state torturers, and so forth). The kinds of categories employed by Camus were never considered. Psychosis or the not-responsible approach was opposed bitterly by those who promoted the old-fashioned virtues, such as responsibility for one's deeds; ignorance, irresistible impulse, and so forth, was no excuse. These kinds of unresolvable conflicts of moral systems required the production of generations of ethics rationalizers as, it seemed, people moved further and further away from religion (as they seem to be moving back again: well, these things come and go in waves).

I ended with a completely un-Camus-like book, being led into astonishing directions and discovering that the world, the real world, was more absurd, crazier, more *ding-an-sichtlich* than any fiction writer, no matter how ingenious and imaginative, could conceive. And, at the same time, without being quite conscious of it, I was also discovering that the social "sciences" were in themselves partially forms of fiction.

In a nutshell, the plot of *Fertig* runs this way: a man, Fertig (this means "finished" in German and Yiddish: I took the name of a college classmate, Howard Fertig, later to become a publisher—we used to jokingly call him Howard's End), marries late in life. He and his wife, social failures with big dreams, are compromising, making the best of a disappointing, loveless life. They have a child, a son. This brings them closer together and, for the first time in their lives, they begin to understand love. One night, the child gets sick. Their doctor cannot be reached (remember that during the period when I was writing the book, doctor-patient relations were changing. Throughout the '50s and early '60s, doctors had been abandoning home visits). The Fertigs give the child aspirin. It doesn't help. They rush their child to the emergency room of a hospital. (As part of my research, refusing to take the mythology of the caring doctor for granted, I went and sat in the emergency rooms of several hospitals to see what went on. I was shocked at the systemic neglect.) By this time the aspirin has taken effect: the child has begun to feel better. The Fertigs are told to take their child home. They decide to go to another hospital. On the way the child has a seizure and dies.

The Fertigs' marriage begins to fall apart. Fertig tries to decide who is responsible for his son's death. Gradually it dawns on him that while there were "whos," the three people, a petty-minded intake worker, a nurse, and a resident, there is a "not-who"; he is in the presence of a larger system of mutually shared responsibility (or, rather, guilt). He wants revenge. But how, after all, does any individual kill a system? He selects exemplary victims . . . seven people, the three who were in the emergency room and four directors of the hospital and decides to kill them and, because his life has fallen apart, he wants to be caught and to have his day in court, perhaps envisioning making a stirring speech..

Further researching the project, I went into several hospitals and walked through them various times during daylight hours and at night to see if I could have access to the personnel so that I, like Fertig, might, if I wanted to, kill them. I found it was quite easy.

But Fertig, naive, becomes a victim of his own illusions. He finds that the criminal justice system, as I found it really to be, and given the complex interaction of the media, is bizarre, surreal. He becomes the victim of half-senile and corrupt judges, ambitious journalists and lawyers, and mutually contradicting psychiatrists with certain stereotypical expectations.

Of course Fertig could not be allowed to have his day in court. By definition, within the context of our society, he had to be a rational, malevolent criminal, possibly a left-wing crazy, or a seriously disturbed individual. If there was reason behind his motivation, it might be if not sympathized with, at least understood. But even to understand Fertig's motivation was to point at the inhuman in society: his complaints about the system that killed his son might fall on receptive ears. Others might take the law into their own hands and do likewise. Juries might choose not to convict. He must be considered psychotic.

Slowly but surely the process drives him insane as, ironically, his corrupt, opportunistic lawyer, to enhance his own reputation, using an insanity-defense plea, begins to regard Fertig—whom he at first considered as a maddened *nebbish*—as a rational and courageous hero. Fertig is remanded to an institution for the criminally insane. He never gets to make his great speech to the world.

Now I have explained this process rationally. What I have not talked about was the way the work consumed me; I worked night and day. There were periods of leaps of insight and periods of slow growth of understanding. I was gradually transformed as I wrote. My view of the world changed yet again.

Fertig was to be rejected twenty-seven times before being published. I went through a period of despair. I began to doubt myself. I wondered . . . is it me or is it them, the editors? I knew, or thought I knew, what made a good book. I began to notice, as I read the various rejection letters, a peculiar phenomenon. If I compiled those parts of the rejection letters in which the editors were critical, or dismissive, my book was completely terrible; if I added up the parts of my book the editors liked, my book was a work of genius.

I decided that, in the meantime, while submitting my book, I would go ahead and write another novel, which was to become *The Warriors*. Now in part the process of *knowing* that an idea is good is completely irrational. No matter how complicated and sophisticated our communication machinery gets, there can be no program that decides on the *rightness* of a creative idea. And mystery of mysteries, the idea of *The Warriors* had lingered in my mind for about fifteen years!

Whereas it had taken more than a year to write *Fertig*, it took me three weeks of intense work, after research, to write *The Warriors*. I could not have done it the way I did without having gone through the growth process in the writing of *Fertig*.

There were a number of steps in the preparation for writing this book. I'm not sure in what order they took place, sequentially or simultaneously. The creative process is a mystery. I conceived the whole plot in one glowing moment. Well, in fact the plot—or rather the motif—had been lying around for thousands of years: the hero journey through adversities, mental or material or both. And the plot of *this* journey was waiting for me for some twenty-four hundred years.

Originally, when the idea had struck me with force years before, I didn't think carefully about the parallels between the ten thousand mercenary Greek soldiers supporting a succession-to-the-throne struggle, a coup (or even call it a revolution), and a potential "army" of social outcasts in our time. I never thought, at the time, to ask myself what made the idea so right. I had learned the value of certain immediate and "unmotivated," what shall I call them, inspirations, which seemed to come out of nowhere. But, at some point, perhaps at that time, perhaps later on, I did begin to wonder if the comparison worked "naturally" or if I was forcing it.

The writer should know when something—the choosing of an image, a simile, the making of a metaphor—is right. But in order to justify the sudden and perfect insight—whether in science, mathematics, or literature—you go back and construct the mental pathway that originally led up to the illumination that seems to have come out of nowhere (in other words, first the effect, which seems to come suddenly out of nowhere, and then the cause). So the question for me, years later, when I was "recollecting in tranquillity," became: What did I see at that particular time in the notion of fighting gangs of the '50s that was in any sense similar to the fate of those Xenephon-led ten thousand ancient Greek mercenary soldiers? I don't know.

Curiously, in our postmodern, poststructural, what have you, time, when the singularity, the absolutely untranslatable uniqueness, of each culture is stressed, I have to note that people—storytellers, poets, writers, memorializers of every kind—in *every* culture, from the most "primitive" to the most "sophisticated," no matter how diverse from any other culture, employ the rhetorical arts. That is to say that the systems of significations, the came-befores, came-afters, is-likes (comparison making, image, simile, and metaphor) and stand-fors (symbol, emblem, synecdoche, etc.), may vary from culture to culture, yet *all* cultures employ the same methodologies as they attempt to represent their internal and external environments. Call this the Thesaurus syndrome because the thing-in-itself, the thing, the experience, the smell, etc., is indescribable and so is-likes are piled on top of is-likes.

If these modes of representation and comparison take place everywhere (and everywhen), are we in the presence of something biological? I believe that bio-chemical-electrical receptors process impulses (translated into need in our minds) that come to us from the outside *and* the inside. This is the way we read . . . no, *we are made* to read the environment. These impulses drive all people. One reads the environment directly or indirectly (in terms of geography and time) using a variety of prosthetic devices (such as, for instance, the writings and ancient relics of others) as if things and forces were very, very close. How, after all, are humans, who are for the most part distanced from direct contact with the nurturing environment, attempting to communicate or describe any "thing in itself," an event or a sensation, a feeling—for instance a smell, or pain—to talk about anything other than in terms of something else, a comparison with some other event, word, thing, sensation, feeling, or sign (or someone else's constructions of signals)?

But there are levels of sensitivity in human consciousness. Whereas most people take their world for granted, some writers, some poets, some language-spinners see certain relationships among people, things, events, or signs of people, things and/or events in a special way, a way that most others cannot or have not seen them.

When I saw the relevance of the two different "texts," fighting gangs and the kid-mercenaries of *The Anabasis*, from two different times, in two different "languages" from two different cultures, to one another I think I saw something no one else had seen. This was not a natural given. So to some extent it had to be forced. This was the question of the choice of mediational ground, the ground of translation. Fundamentally, there are two kinds of mediational grounds; and *inter*cultural (of course there are many more interacting levels). *Inter*cultural "texts" should, according to the postmodernists, be exclusive, untranslatable, and inviolate (which doesn't stop people from violating and translating). But by forcing incommensurables (referencing them, indexing them) onto the mediational ground of his or her choosing (influenced by the context of a received culture), the artist (or, for that matter, the social and psychological "scientist") colonizes and conquers all "texts." Intellectual imperialism? Of a sort. And, after all, isn't the writer a kind of spy?

In retrospect I suppose that in my mind the immediate mediational ground upon which fighting gangs met *The Anabasis* was a publication of that time, *Classic Comics*. (The very publication of this periodical constituted an act of expropriation.) This periodical presented great works of literature such as *The Iliad* or the adventures of the Argonauts (but never *The Anabasis,* which was too esoteric, but would have made a great comic book). Somehow, in my imagination *Classic Comics*—possibly the only material gang members might have read—could have presented the Greek warriors as the kind of heroic cartoon figures with whom they might have identified.

To make my parallel fit, I invented a gang leader—Ismael Rivera (reference here to the rebellious and Young American critic hero of *Moby-Dick*, but taken a step further)—who envisioned the

198

possibility of organizing all of the gangs of New York into one huge semirevolutionary army. Of course I "invented" nothing. There were, in fact, several gang leaders who not only had that vision but also had what one could call "native" organizational genius; they were "instinctive" theoreticians. My "hero" replicated the "Cyrus" of Xenephon's history. He would send word to all corners of the city, summoning plenipotentiaries of all the city's gangs for a grand, revolutionary meeting.

I chose to tell the major part of the story from the perspective of, first, a small, insignificant gang and then from the point of view of one of its members, Hinton (I had already invented him in a short story). This gang would make the journey up from the projects in Coney Island to the meeting ground in the Bronx (Van Courtlandt Park, or call it Babylon) and then back. The representatives, after the whole venture had been broken up by the police, would seek refuge in Woodlawn Cemetery (where, incidentally, Melville was buried) and then they would have to, like the Greek ten thousand, fight their way through hostile territories ruled by other gangs to their home grounds. The escape from the cemetery is of course a kind of resurrectionary move. Like the Greeks, they would finally reach the "Black Sea," only, in this case, it was the Atlantic Ocean off Coney Island. Thus also the sea, considering the hero's last position, curled up with his thumb in his mouth, to be a "return" to the womb, having gained much knowledge, and in the light shining on the sea, he has, indeed, returned to a grave again.

Since I had gone through the writing of *Fertig*, I was determined to construct a true reflection (!) of the real world through which my literary gangs would move, the world of New York City as it really is, with its streets and subways. Could they do it; could they assemble without being spotted? I decided that I had to actually traverse the distances via subways in order to time the journey (this included walking through the tunnel between 96th Street on the West Side and the next stop, 110th Street: scary).

199

And yet, since I wanted to fold in the mythic and ritual, to make this journey a rite of passage, I thought in terms of similar (anthropological and literary) rite-of-passage journeys. Yet, whatever I thought about rhetorical devices, parallels, literary references, I was determined to bury them in such a way that they would work subliminally on the minds of the literate reader. If you missed the references, then you had, I hoped, a good story.

I, through the intermediation of several friends who worked in probation and parole, contacted some gang members and began to interview them. My interviews didn't go well. I began to feel that I was being told what the gang-members thought I wanted to hear; a common phenomenon anthropologists and social workers faced. I had to find some way to observe them without being observed myself; in short, to spy. (As I said above, all sociologists and anthropologists are spies.) My solution was to hire a small, beat-up panel truck, punch little holes in the sides, park the truck on the gangs' turf during the early morning, get in the truck, and just watch and listen. I was trying to capture the jargon, the rhythms of speech, the body English (or is it *ganglish*?), and so forth, if I could. (Even as I was trying to practice what Keats called negative capability, the well-known and omnipresent Heisenberg effect was always operative; indeterminacy was part of mine and everyone's mind.)

Gangs (of the time I was writing about) were quite different than the gangs of today. For one thing, automobiles were not available to them. For another, there were very few guns around. The gangs were neighborhood-bound and quite ignorant of the city outside their own territories; indeed, they were frightened of strange turf. Whatever contacts, alliances, conflicts, and permissions to travel through alien lands belonging to other gangs took place were conducted through their leaders. They practiced diplomacy from gang to gang, albeit in crude language, but, formally, just like the diplomacy conducted by nations. It's fascinating to see these social forms spring up among the "ignorant" "lower" social strata; no readers of Kissinger they . . . and yet they had the same sophisticated understanding.

Economically the gangs of those times were totally marginal. They had just about no entrée into organized crime. The very need to form gangs was a product of their irrelevance. This situation has changed enormously, fueled by the drug trade, which brings neighborhood localities into contact with the global economy, requiring new, sophisticated modes of understanding and operation. And, as with all trade conflicts over control of markets from time immemorial, disputes require heavy weaponry, which is easily available.

I read in the sketchy history of gangs (after all, they don't leave records); they were a universal phenomenon; even ancient Athens had its youth gangs. Gangs bud off from the so-called main body of society. This, it seems to me, is an almost natural, even bio-evolutionary happening, even now, in these days, as a protest, conscious or unconscious, against the homogenization of global-ization. The structure of the street gangs tended to be like Latin American dictatorships in which the pragmatic and formal were melded into an amalgam of the military, tribal, and familial . . . a sort of organism. Many gangs rejected their own families and made their own. Since the laws of society around them did not apply in the streets, leadership was determined by force and/or cunning: any leader's reign was always chancy. And yet these leadership maneuverings and fights were like the struggles for control on the national and international level. If one looks closely at *any* government structure, from the so-called democratic—as in our own country—to the so-called totalitarian, one sees constant internecine warfare, usually referred to as bureaucratic infighting. After all, how many routes to power are there? As it was and is with "legitimate" governments, so it was, and is, with the gangs. Violence was the final arbiter.

I decided to use my own variant of this tripartite structure in my book. I added something that, at first glance, seemed alien. I had been reading the classic Chinese novel called *At Water Margin* (incidentally, one of Mao's favorite books, although I didn't know that at the time). This novel tells the story of a band of heroes, some of whom are criminals, others revolutionary. They combine to overthrow the emperor. What interested me about the book was the combination of ritual language, the use of overpolite honorifics (this unworthy second son honors his elder brother, or uncle . . . etc.), as well as the horrific violence with which they did one another in. I made my subject gang use this familial mode of address.

When I had assembled my material, I had to decide on my structure. At first I laid out the story chronologically. Then I decided that it didn't work. I then began on a note of suspense and puzzlement . . . the hook, so to speak. After the grand meeting— although the reader doesn't know this yet—is broken up by the police, our subject gang has fled. We meet them huddled in Woodlawn Cemetery. We then flash back to the beginning and lead up to the events just before we meet our gang . . . and then proceed forward. My choice of order was the well-known and ancient *in medias res* strategy. In fact, every story in the world begins this way, including the folk tale of the cosmic Big Bang that putatively starts the universe. Something always comes before. And at some point in any story, the what-came-before is either taken for granted and understood by the audience, or must be explained. Let me note in passing that there is no problem with the flashback in literature but it causes trouble in films.

The meeting itself was modeled after the great, Lucifer-led council, the pandemonium—all demons—in *Paradise Lost*, about another failed revolt (the gangs in my book were given names from Milton's epic . . . Thrones, Dominations, etc.). I was connecting Ismael Rivera to Lucifer, who also made his speech in the darkness of hell. What I meant to imply—the subtext, as it were—was that my gang, after its revolt against the "divine" order of things, has fallen to the lowest possible depths and must "ascend" to their homeland (think *Divine Comedy* or Zola's *Germinal*). This reflected the traditional myth/ritual of the descent into hell and the ascent to a kind of heaven, which turns out to be miserable.

In planning, I employed a corporate management tool called PERT . . . Program Evaluation and Review Technique. Assembling a business enterprise or a story requires the same kind of planning. I made a grid. On the top of the grid, in each box, I placed the time plus each step of the plot. On the side of the grid I placed various things, which would serve as running, extended metaphors. I followed the progress of these things through the long night . . . such as the gradual disintegration of a shoe, the change in the weather, and so forth. These things also mirrored the psychic state of the characters as they were on their "long march" from the Bronx to Coney Island.

Now although this methodology seems very mechanical, very, how should I put it, anticreative (inspirational), at the same time I believed that one should prepare the ground carefully so as to always be ready to encounter the unexpected that is only revealed as the writing continues . . . much like an athlete practices in order to be ready for the contingent that is always part of life, as it is, if the writer is not too rigid, in the act of writing. Many times I have said to myself something like, "Oh, that's what he, or she, is like."

Since it was to be an attempted revolution, I chose that most patriotic of all days, July Fourth. Perhaps this choice of revolution and date reflected my relation to this country in which I was born . . . a fundamental hostility that is more than political, also part of my psychology. (And yet, at the time of the writing I was not consciously political because, in 1939, when the Hitler-Stalin pact was signed, I became apolitical . . . until the later '60s. My *conscious* involvement with politics came *after* writing *The Warriors*.

Fertig was still circulating and being rejected as I was writing my second book. However, unknown to me, there had been editors who had been in different publishing houses who had read it and wanted to take it on but didn't have the clout to do so. As they changed jobs, they had come together at Holt, Rinehart and Winston, into a sort of critical mass. They read *The Warriors* and agreed to publish it. I was to work with one of them who was enthusiastic about my book.

Now that my book was to be published, perhaps my other book, *Fertig*—I thought of it as the more serious work—would be taken on, depending, of course, on the success of *The Warriors*. I was not alarmed when my editor said that he thought that a few editorial changes should be made. However, when I got the manuscript back, there were at least five to ten changes per page. Was this the book the editor liked so much? The fight began.

Consider my state of mind. I had been submitting works for years; my work had been praised but no editor had taken it on. If I resisted the changes, would I be jeopardizing publication? And yet I fought, page by page, even including the number of times the word "fuck" occurred. (The editing process took place in 1963–64, before the great linguistic, sexual, and political climacteric of the '60s. *Last Exit to Brooklyn* had been shocking; publishing houses censored through the editorial process.)

In addition, we had a very big quarrel over the last chapter of the book. My protagonist, Hinton, comes home after a night of adventure and terror. As he walks through his apartment, he passes a bed where one of his half brothers is sleeping with one of his half sisters (from three fathers); the description was quite casual . . . almost, as it were, in passing; no big deal. My outraged editor asked how I could violate that great taboo, common to all societies, oh dreaded word and worse, act, incest (he forgot, of course, Egypt, and even Corinth—an aside; Oedipus was "from" Corinth—and other cultures)? I pointed out that in the first place, the couple was sleeping together, not fucking. Space was limited. But in the second

204

place, incest was, in my experience, not unusual among my clients. (This was an elitist assumption on my part. I was wrong. Incest is also common in middle-class families, to say nothing of upper-class families.) I refused to change it. My editor kept saying, "Well, Sol, if you want to ruin your own book . . ." Very scary. I persisted. The editor did, in part, prevail; one "fuck" was excised. The book remained as I had submitted it.

My editor did serve one useful, indeed vital, function: he chose the introductory quotes from Xenephon. At the time I couldn't realize how important these quotes were to the making of the reputation of the book. Without these quotes, how would anyone know about its classical parallel. (If one didn't know about the parallel between *Ulysses* and the *Odyssey*, would it have gotten on the college reading lists?)

Despite the fact that the printing was small, surprisingly *The Warriors* got national attention. What was more surprising was that so many people had even decided to review what might have been just another book about "juvenile delinquents." The review in *The Nation* was favorable. The critic had one important reservation; he thought that the analogy to *The Anabasis* was perhaps a little too forced, even contemptuous of one of the Greek classics. After all, this was Greek civilization I was talking about. Well, at least the reviewer had not only heard about *The Anabasis* but had actually read it. What, I thought, were those mercenaries (kids, really) but the result of overpopulation whereas, in this country (this was before the escalation in Vietnam), there was no use for our indigenous poor young people. And after all, were the Greeks really so noble?

I determined that my next novel (actually the previous one, *Fertig*) would go to another publisher. I later found out that an important stockholder in Holt was so incensed by the book's content that he wanted it removed from the market.

The Warriors was picked up and published in England and, of all places, Japan, which, of course, did not have these problems . . . or so I thought.

And now a period of hiatus came once again. While my reputation was established and reinforced by the publication of *Fertig,* I thought that was the end of *The Warriors.* What I didn't know was that several movie producers had considered making the book into a movie, among them, Otto Preminger, of all people. I ran into another producer who was interested in the book. He told me how much he liked the book. But the only thing that bothered him was that he—a man undergoing psychoanalysis—couldn't understand the psychology of the kids. I didn't tell him that I didn't understand them either.

The years passed; I wrote other books. Then, 1976—or 1977, I don't remember exactly—I got an offer from a small, independent filmmaker to make a movie out of *The Warriors.* He told me that he had always loved the book and had long wanted to produce it. He said he could do it almost exactly as it had been written. I was excited. However, at the very last moment, in fact the day before signing, my agent received an offer for the rights to the novel offered by a Hollywood producer, Lawrence Gordon. The movie would be directed by Walter Hill. I agreed to the more lucrative offer. I would get more money but more important, perhaps my book would be republished.

What I didn't know was that, at the time, a kind of collective madness had seized Hollywood; a number of gang movies were scheduled to be made at the same time by different studios. As it would turn out, the first to make it to the screen would be *The Warriors.*

After the signing, months went by; I heard nothing. Then one spring day I read in the newspapers that Lawrence Gordon and Walter Hill had come to New York to film the movie. The newspaper article happened to mention the name of the hotel where Gordon was staying. I wanted to see some of the filming. On an impulse, I telephoned the hotel and asked for Gordon's room. I introduced myself, giving my name. He was puzzled; he didn't know who I was. I told him I was the author of *The Warriors*. Immediately, to my surprise, Gordon went into what seemed like a canned rap to the outraged author who feels that his sacred work of art is about to be philistinized. Even worse, the author might ask for some part in the production of the movie. Gordon said that this was to be an action movie, an adventure story, and that a movie was different from a novel. What this *spiel* reflected was the traditional conflict between writers on the one hand and actors, directors, producers, and studios on the other.

All of which I already knew. I knew what the industry was about. I kept trying to interrupt, attempting to say that all I wanted was to see the filming. Finally Gordon told me where the next day's filming would take place . . . in Riverside Park, at night. The scene to be filmed was the grand meeting of the gangs.

When I got to the location that night, there were hundreds of young men and some women. I was overwhelmed and thought that here was my imagination concretized, industrialized, and populated with living people.

I introduced myself to Walter Hill. He immediately went into the same rap Gordon had given me. Once again, trying to deal with this industry-wide anxiety, I kept trying to interrupt. When we got that straightened out, Hill told me where to stand and watch. What I was seeing were the moments when the leader was trying to unify the gangs (Ismael Rivera in my book; Cyrus in the film . . . someone had done their xenophobic homework). He makes his speech. The police break up the grand, revolutionary meeting. The actor was awful, the dialogue lame; Hill had no idea how the street kids really talked.

I was fascinated by the difference between what I had tried to do in the book and the way the film tried to deal with the problem of the grand assemblage of gang representatives. In the book I dealt with the technology of a single man trying to reach hundreds of people in a large, open space. In the book, the message is spoken in a normal way and relayed from gang to gang. As it is relayed, the message gradually entropizes (think of the game of telephone). In the movie the problem was solved by a grand speech to the assembled multitude in which all can hear the speech-maker clearly.

Months passed; I heard nothing of the course of the production from anyone associated with the film. All I could do was wait to be informed of the opening. I did hear from a friend who was in the industry: he told me that there had been a preview in San Francisco and it was badly received. Perhaps it would never reach the screen.

Then six months later, suddenly, I began to see posters on the subway stations. I saw coming attractions on television. But no one had thought to inform me of the opening directly.

Paramount was distributing the film; I decided to call their publicity office. I introduced myself, told them I was the author of the book. They asked if I wanted to go to the premiere. Again, apparently no one had thought of informing me. I got three tickets; for myself, my wife, and my daughter.

The premiere was held in one of the big theaters in Times Square (this was before the theaters were split into smaller ones). When I arrived I saw Walter Hill in the lobby; he was trembling. His last film had been a flop: his reputation was riding on this one.

I looked for my novel on the screen. I found the skeleton of it intact. Its revolutionary content was missing; no Fourth of July. The first three minutes—the gathering of the fighting-gang bands into an army of revolt—showed what cinematic compression at its best could do; almost perfect. "Almost perfect?" Not totally. For me, the most thrilling moment came when my name, as author of the book upon which the film was based, came shooting out of the subway tunnel darkness, filling the screen.

In the movie the Warriors were racially mixed; almost an impossibility. My warriors had all been black. The hero of the

208

movie story was white. (I have to admit that I doubt the movie would have been as popular—back then in 1979, the date of its release—if the protagonist were black.) The ending promises the potentiality of happiness . . . if the protagonist and the woman, who may become his girlfriend, change their ways. The movie, whose action was more balletic than real, was much less violent than my novel; the casual, random killing of a bystanding man and the gang rape had been excised (well, how could you relate to a gang that did such things). I thought, on the whole, that the movie was trashy, although beautifully filmed.

I noticed one thing that was at first a little puzzling: a sheriff appears for a few frames. There was a scene in the book in which the hero, Hinton, in his flight from the Bronx to Brooklyn, wanders through an arcade (long since demolished) in the Forty-second Street subway station. There he sees a kind of automated sheriff. For a quarter you could stage a gunfight with him. The sheriff, would, in his prerecorded voice, tell you to get out of town or he would kill you. In the book, Hinton takes on the sheriff. In the movie, you see the sheriff but nothing comes of it. The apparition is puzzling. Walter Hill had obviously filmed my scene but had cut almost all of it out. I was also annoyed that the subway stations where Hill filmed the action were out of sequence or simply unused. Small complaint.

Because I must have been groaning during the showing, my daughter, Susanna, who was fourteen at the time, assured me that the kids would love it, and so they did. It certainly made her reputation in our neighborhood.

As I was about to leave the theater, one of Paramount's publicity people brought me to meet a critic for, I think, public television: I can't remember his name. He didn't care for the movie. He said, however, that he had heard that *The Warriors* was based on a Greek classic; perhaps *The Odyssey*? (How did he know this? The film didn't indicate the parallel. Had the public relations people mentioned this in their promotional literature?) I mentioned the source, *The Anabasis*, which he did not know. I quickly told him the story of that failed usurpation-revolution. As I talked, I could see his attitude was changing. Clearly, now that the critic had a great classic parallel—which elevated this sordid, modern-day story—he could give it a good review.

I went home, disappointed. The next day, opening day, I was invited to Paramount's publicity department. There were a number of journalists there. One of them asked me what I thought about the movie. I disliked it but I didn't want to say that. I said instead that I found it "interesting." I was immediately taken aside by one of the publicity people who told me that the word "interesting," was the kiss of death. I tried to avoid talking to anyone else.

In the meantime, the actors were being interviewed. I detected a kind of party line. All of them denied that the movie was about violence for violence's sake. Rather, they said, one and all, that it was a movie about family.

A number of things happened next. First, a friend went to see the movie and telephoned me to say that not only was the show sold out, but also the next one; the line went around the block. I also heard that on the night of general release, a movie house somewhere in Kansas was sold out again and again in the midst of a blinding snowstorm. The movie was to push *Star Wars* out from first place.

I received a phone call from Pauline Kael; she also had heard that the movie and my book were based on a classic; perhaps again Homer? I mentioned *The Anabasis*. She wanted to know if my book was a reference to the French poet St. John Perse's *Anabase*? I told her that although I had read the poem (in reality a few lines, and in English, not French)—a little one-upmanship—I explained my book's real "source," telling Ms. Kael the whole story. And, as I told her the tale, I could sense that her excitement was growing; at last, a hook for intellectuals upon which to hang her review in *The New Yorker*. It was not only a glowing review, but she had also taken the trouble to read my book and mentioned it, glowingly.

Later Paramount would take out a full-page ad in *The New York Times* with the complete *New Yorker* review, giving the movie the proper cachet.

But outside the professional-intellectual level, the movie had already captured the imaginations of the kids, including many gang members, in a different way. Many young men, now in their thirties and forties, have told me that seeing the movie (again and again and again) had been a defining moment in their young lives.

And then I heard that fights had broken out among young men waiting to see the movie. Someone, in Los Angeles, I think, had been shot and killed. And there were other "alarming" acts of violence. My phone began to ring (and would continue for the next two weeks . . . night and day); reporters were calling to ask if I, the original creator of the idea, the *demiurgos*, as it were, felt at all responsible for the death and the violence. Of course I denied this. I hadn't made the movie.

I have to admit that secretly I felt—a thought I would never express in public—that the violence and the controversy surrounding the movie would help sell the movie, thus generating demand for the reprinting of my book, which it did. The book was not only republished in the United States, England and Japan (a new translation), but also in France (almost banned), Germany, Spain, Italy (printed by three different publishers: I was later to learn that many young Italians felt that, because of the movie, they now understood the United States perfectly), and Portugal.

As far as the media was concerned, the events led it to create a climate of alarm. There were reports that various gangs had begun to copy the style of the Warriors. Graffiti bearing the name of Warriors began to appear (some of the graffiti had of course been spray-painted by the filmmakers). Some theaters refused to show the movie as well as the other gang movies when they were released.

Unbeknownst to me, Paramount called in a number of behavioral scientists to see how they might lessen the impact of those images deemed evocative of violence. But, in fact, what were these? How did they work on the "susceptible" minds of the viewers? While it is true that where, for instance, advertising attempts to manipulate the minds of people, it is not always possible to pick out the one, or set of images, in the context of a movie story, that will lead to an act of violence. Other movies about gangs hadn't done that. On the other hand, the influence of *The Godfather* on certain aspects of the real Mafia is legendary. It is only after the fact that social psychologists can "determine" what it was that affected so many young people.

It was clear that nothing could be cut from the movie; it was already too tight to take out anything. It was decided to drop all advertising. It seemed as though the movie had disappeared from the screen, although it was still showing all over the country. Of course the audience numbers dropped.

What is astonishing to me is the durability of the movie. It was released some twenty years ago. There is an Internet Web site devoted to it. New members come online all the time. It has become, in the parlance of media when they can't understand the why of the development of a social phenomenon, a "cult" movie. It certainly made Walter Hill's reputation. I have to admit that I didn't and still don't understand the phenomenon. There hasn't been one film made in the United States that I would consider seeing five times, as many who loved the film version of *The Warriors* did.

The Warriors is not the best of my books. It was out of print and more or less unknown to the lovers of the movie. Yet, without the book, there would be no film. I find that amusing.